DEEP THREAT

DEEP THREAT

A BILLY BECKETT NOVEL

BY
SCOTT PRATT

WITH KELLY HODGE

This book is dedicated to the memory of Scott Pratt, my late friend and literary mentor, who believed that nothing in life is beyond imagination and went about proving it every day. He was a remarkable storyteller with great vision and drive. Our collaboration on the Billy Beckett series of novels was among his final active projects before departing this earth, and it will remain a bittersweet postscript for me personally. I take solace in knowing that Scott's indomitable spirit lives on in family and friends, and in the many compelling adventures he brought to life for his readers.

K.H.

This book, along with every book I've written and every book I'll write, is dedicated to my darling Kristy, to her unconquerable spirit, and to her inspirational courage. She lost her 11-year battle with breast cancer on June 23, 2018. She fought like a lioness to her last breath. I loved her before I was born, and I'll love her after I'm long gone.

PROLOGUE

Charles Ratliff was sweating profusely as he stooped in an old sugarcane field on the outskirts of New Orleans, a shovel in his blistered hands. He wasn't wearing a shirt and his body glistened in the bright sunshine. His baggy jeans were dirty and stained, his tennis shoes the same color as the brown soil he was moving. He'd been digging for a while and was breathing heavily.

"Speed it up, Charles. It's getting near noon, and we're hungry. You're getting close, but that hole ain't near deep enough yet."

The man who was overseeing the digging looked at his wristwatch. He laughed like he often did at the end of these assignments. He took a perverted pleasure in watching a soon-to-be corpse assist in his own demise.

"Charles was never good at anything except finding drugs and trouble," he said to his partner, who was stone-faced and leaning against a black SUV with a Glock 42 .380 pistol poised at his side. The overseer was short, balding, and thick. His puffy face was covered with a dark stubble of beard. He was wearing a white polo, khaki pants and a pair of black Sperry boat shoes. "We could put that on his grave marker, but he isn't going to have one." He spread his hands dramatically. "I can picture it in my mind. 'Here lies Charles, a pathetic loser.'"

The man cackled again.

Charles wiped his brow and kept digging without saying a word. He was more than knee deep in the hole, and the mound of rich Louisiana dirt was piling up beside him.

Finally, the short man said, "Okay, drop the shovel and get on your knees. Let's see how you fit."

***

The gravity of the situation hadn't been apparent a few hours earlier, at least not to Charles. He was just another shiftless addict looking for his next high when the men surprised him and grabbed him up in a back alley of the French Quarter. Charles knew he shouldn't have returned to the Big Easy, because he had crossed Frank Romano, and Romano was looking to get even. But New Orleans was the city Charles had drifted to for years, and he knew all the places he could score dope.

As he was led into an abandoned warehouse down on the waterfront, Charles wondered how he could make things right and walk away. The mood was grim, but maybe Charles could talk Romano down. Maybe he could reason with the man.

The office door opened. At the end of a long table sat a hulking figure with dark, slicked-back hair and a bushy goatee. His shirt was spotted with perspiration, and a thick gold chain hung around his neck. Charles knew Romano was a made mob guy, and he looked the part. He was a walking stereotype. A menacing scowl radiated from Romano's face.

Charles also knew Romano was the head of a growing crime syndicate that had been running drugs all along the Gulf Coast and leaving plenty of carnage in its wake. The two henchmen who had snatched Charles off the street stood watch at the door.

"Sit down," Romano said. Tiny beads of sweat shined on his forehead as he lit a cigarette.

"Want one, Charles?"

"No, sir. I don't smoke."

Romano glanced at his men and snorted. "That's funny. Son of a bitch has every bad habit known to man, but he don't smoke." He looked back at Charles. "This might be a good time to start."

Charles remained silent. He tried to allow his mind to take him to a different time and place, back when he was young and sturdy and athletic – a tight end, in fact, and a good one. He could have led a different life had he chosen to use the athletic ability that had been bestowed upon him by God or nature or whatever. But he hadn't. He'd made bad choices, especially when it came to substance abuse, and he looked at least ten years older than fifty-one. It now appeared he might not see fifty-two, and the end would probably be ugly.

"Do you know why you're here?" Romano said.

"I guess it's because of my son. I tried to talk to him – me and his mother both tried – but he don't listen no more. That guy, that sports agent, has been controlling him for a while."

"So the young man is a big star now and doesn't want to make new friends? We're just trying to help him, Charles. Trying to put him on the right path for the future so he doesn't make the same mistakes you made. We were counting on your influence."

Charles swallowed hard. "I know. I can still help."

The crime boss exhaled a billowing cloud of smoke that seemed to fill the room and tapped his fingertips impatiently on the table.

"The biggest problem, Charles, is that I invested in you. I gave you something of value. I gave you precise instructions on how to handle this valuable thing. And what happened? You stole my investment, and you delivered nothing in return. You made me look like a fool."

"I tried to do what you wanted, Mr. Romano. I swear it. I talked to the brother. I did everything I could."

"Bullshit. Did you deliver the package like you were told? It was a simple job. You were the one to suggest it, right? You said you knew this guy, that for an ounce of blow he could get in your son's ear and change his mind. Isn't that what you said?"

"I saw the man in Florida and he said he'd do what he could," Charles said. "I left the package in his hands. That was it."

"Stop insulting my intelligence, Charles, or I'm going to shoot you where you sit. I hear everything that goes on out there on the street, and what I hear is that you didn't follow my instructions. You were selfish. You stole part of what was in my package. You took care of *you*. You doomed yourself for a few grams of blow."

"I'm sorry," Charles said. "Let me make it up to you. I'll pay you for the coke I took. I'll talk to my boy again. I'll get him to bring Jarvis around."

"That's what you said last time." Romano snuffed out his cigarette and turned to his men. "I've wasted enough time and money on this junkie," he said. "Get him out of here. And make sure I don't see him again. Then put out the word that you don't steal from Frank Romano, and if you tell him you're going to do something, you better deliver. Make an example out of him."

***

The grave was now deep enough. The stocky man walked over and told Charles to kneel in the middle of the hole. He raised his pistol, a Smith & Wesson M&P 9mm, and cocked the hammer.

Charles Ratliff hit his knees, heard the metallic click, took a deep breath, and looked up at the cloudless sky. He thought fleetingly of what a waste his life had been. Then he bowed his head.

Two bullets shattered his skull, and he slumped into the hole – a perfect fit – as a crimson mist settled over him.

PART I

CHAPTER ONE

J arvis Thompson could catch anything thrown his way, and he could run like the wind. Football was his great escape.

Down in the Florida panhandle, they called him "The Autumn Blaze" – a tribute to the wide receiver's breathtaking speed and the dusty little town where his story began. The nickname followed him to college, and it would fit nicely in the NFL, too, because Jarvis was going to compete on the fastest fields of all.

The folks in Autumn, Florida, would be mighty proud.

"I can't wait," Jarvis said, gazing down at another sleek cabin cruiser as it meandered past the gray, contemporary home that sat high above the Tennessee River. "I'm going to be the whole package, man, going to do everything we've talked about. Scoring touchdowns and posing in the end zone. Commercials. All that stuff.

You'll make sure it happens, won't you, Billy?"

A beaming smile crossed the face of his mentor. Billy Beckett had his own dreams about Jarvis's future. Big dreams. They'd started back in the early days, when the kid was just making a name for himself in the football-crazy Sunshine State, before every college powerhouse in the country lusted after him. The dreams had only grown more real as the years unfolded.

Most everyone around the game had heard Jarvis Thompson's all-too-familiar backstory by now. As a black child growing up in government-subsidized housing in Autumn, Florida, he'd survived all kinds of hell – lowlife father, alcoholic mother, girlfriend shot dead in the yard, the gangs and drugs. But Jarvis had eventually fought his way out. The only part of the backstory most people didn't know was that Billy had played a major role in making it happen.

And now, finally, it seemed the stars were lining up just right for both of them.

The possibilities were intoxicating as the men sat on the veranda of Billy's house, sipping Red Bull on a pristine fall afternoon. At that moment, Billy felt more like a big brother than a young sports agent closing in on his most high-profile client yet. He was the only reason Jarvis had come to Knoxville, and he was satisfied with the way it was all playing out.

"If you think you've gotten a lot of attention here, Jarvis, just wait," he said. "The NFL is the greatest show on turf, and it's all about quarterbacks and receivers, guys like you. The best thing is that you're better than most. You're bigger, you're faster, you have incredible hands. And you're an intelligent young man. We just have to get you through this season healthy. After that, there's nothing standing in our way."

Billy took a long sip of his drink and continued: "The whole world is going to know about Jarvis Thompson. I *will* make sure of it."

The experts said Jarvis would go early in the draft, maybe in the top three. At six-foot-four and two hundred and twenty pounds, with strong, sinewy hands that gripped those leather spirals like a vise and elite footspeed, he was already an All-American at the University of Tennessee. The program had been a launching pad to the pros for so many at his position through the years that they called it Wide Receiver U, and Jarvis might have been the best the school had ever produced.

His celebrity was growing as he approached two hundred career catches. Fans would hang around the stadiums in clusters long after the games, just to get a closer glimpse of this freak of nature with the bright smile. Wherever Jarvis landed in the NFL, the endorsement deals were sure to follow.

The Autumn Blaze was more than halfway through his junior season now, a battle-hardened, twenty-one-year-old used to carrying a heavy load. Even on a mediocre team, he was leading the conference in receptions and touchdowns for the second straight year. If things just stayed on track, he would leave Knoxville as a player whose legend would only continue to grow.

Sometimes Jarvis thought about the good he'd be able to do for others. He'd build his grandmother a new home, for starters. She had once taken him in, protected him when he was vulnerable, before moving away. He knew both his mother and father would come around with their hands out, but he wasn't yet certain what he would do for them. They'd done nothing for him other than bringing him into the world. They'd been a constant source of irritation once they realized Jarvis might be a potential gold mine, but he tried to keep from thinking about them too much. He would eventually do right by them. He just wasn't sure what the right thing was.

He was a young man, though, one who had lived his life in abject poverty, and the possibility of becoming an instant millionaire inside of a year also caused him to daydream about some other things.

"I'm gonna buy a fast car, first thing," Jarvis said to Billy. "Probably a red one. I'll get a big house with a pool. Maybe a boat like yours, only bigger."

Billy raised his eyebrows. "Bigger, huh? I guess you'll want my girlfriend, too."

"That one may be a little too fast for me. I'm not sure I could handle Rachel."

"Believe me, you couldn't," Billy said, chuckling as he got up and walked into the house. He emerged a few minutes later with the morning's *Knoxville Journal*, pulled out the sports section and pointed to the lead story.

"Right now, you just worry about Alabama," he said. "Hell, you were playing Pop Warner ball down in Autumn the last time Tennessee beat those guys. I had just gotten out of school here. If you want to leave this school as a real hero, catch a bunch of passes and spank their butts this weekend. Twelve losses in a row is more than enough."

Billy had always spoken in a straightforward manner, and Jarvis had always listened.

Jarvis smiled and pulled back the dreads from his broad shoulders, looping a black elastic band around them. His eyes darted from the dark green water below to the azure sky above and the large maples that had exploded with color all around.

"Momma is supposed to be here this weekend," he said. "And she isn't too happy. Still wants me to sit down with those guys from New Orleans. She says nothing is official yet."

"Are we talking about this Sonny Bradley guy again?" Billy said. "I thought it was just a formality now between you and me. I thought we understood and trusted each other. You can't officially sign with me yet, but as far as I'm concerned, it's a done deal. What's there to talk about?"

"Bradley's guys have been coming around the house and putting ideas in her head. You know she never wanted me to come up here to begin with."

Billy's eyes narrowed and he snatched the key to his Escalade off the table. The disgust he felt was familiar. He'd heard it all before.

"But you *did* come up here, and you did the right thing," he said. "I have some business in Atlanta tomorrow, but we'll talk again soon. We need to get this settled, once and for all, and move on. Now, let's get you back to campus."

CHAPTER TWO

Billy smiled. He could tell the huge man was nervous. Leroy Mitchell was surrounded in the middle of a car enthusiast's wonderland. Exotic beasts were scattered all around the lot – Ferraris, Lamborghinis, Lotuses, Aston Martins.

Billy didn't think Leroy knew much about any of that. He drove a Ford pickup.

The left offensive tackle, the man who protected the quarterback's "blind side," was one of the Atlanta Falcons' most popular players, and today that was all that mattered. His natural, country-boy charm and his sheer physical presence on camera – he stood six-foot-eight and weighed three hundred and thirty pounds – would carry the commercial for SuperCars Unlimited just fine.

SuperCars was an iconic business for men with an excess of two things – testosterone and expendable income. There were many such men in the Atlanta metroplex, and the owner paid pro athletes, especially Falcons, to put a rugged, appealing face on his advertising.

For the moment, that face belonged to Leroy Mitchell, who just happened to be one of Billy's favorite clients.

"I told you we'd make you a television star," Billy said with a laugh as they waited for a producer to bring the short script. "You'd make triple the money if you were a quarterback, but this is still a good gig. Shows off your personality."

"I hope I can read this stuff without stuttering," Mitchell said. "Just being around these cars makes me nervous. I wouldn't even fit in most of them, and I wouldn't know how to drive them if I did."

"So you wouldn't trade that pickup for one? I'm sure we could work out a deal this morning."

"Why don't I just keep the truck and put that little yellow number over there in the bed and take it home to the wife? I can see her face now when I pull into the driveway."

"She'd be happy?" Billy said.

"I'm kidding. She'd kill me. She's a pickup kind of girl."

"Careful," Billy said. "What you just said could be open to interpretation."

"Say what?"

"Never mind."

The producer, a mid-twenties guy with a manicured, dark beard and shoulder-length hair, walked up and everyone snapped to attention. "All right, Leroy," he said, "let's do this."

Billy slapped his man on the shoulder and faded into the background. He was comfortable there, on the edge of the action. He had a vested interest, sure, but he'd never believed in being overbearing, and he didn't seek the spotlight.

It had been five years since Billy left a thriving Atlanta law firm to blaze his own trail as a sports agent. The lure of guiding elite athletes through their fantasy worlds was too tempting for the ambitious attorney from the Smoky Mountains to resist.

At thirty-six years old, he was becoming a force for the players he represented, slowly but surely.

"Just stand there and look big, Leroy," Billy said as the cameramen moved in. "Don't think too much. It isn't good for you."

"Excuse me, guys," Leroy said, "but would you mind if I pancaked my agent on the pavement before we get started?"

The producer laughed. "Hold on," he said. "I want to get that on camera. Maybe we can work it into the commercial."

Mitchell was among two dozen of Billy's clients in the NFL. The fourth-round pick out of Auburn had more than exceeded expectations in his three seasons with the Falcons, earning a starting job and positioning himself for a major raise when his rookie contract expired. He was also increasingly in demand by regional advertisers looking for a good-natured giant.

Billy had driven down for the commercial shoot just to make sure everything went smoothly, and, more importantly, to make sure that everyone was happy.

That appeared to be the case as the small production crew got ready to pack up. The business owner was smiling and holding an autographed football, talking about the Tampa Bay game that weekend and promising more promotional work. The lineman took home five grand for his trouble. The meager percentage Billy would receive would barely pay his expenses for making the drive, but that didn't matter. What mattered was that everyone had a good experience.

"That wasn't too bad," Mitchell said. "Thanks for lining it up, Billy. Let me take you to dinner later on."

"I'd like to, but I have to get back to Knoxville. It's Alabama week."

Mitchell let out a hearty laugh.

"I know that week, big time," he said. "Everybody in the state of Alabama went crazy when I was at Auburn and we played them. Some dude from Dadeville even came over and poisoned two oak trees on Toomer's Corner after we beat them one year. At least we beat the Tide occasionally. Your Tennessee boys can't say the same."

Billy was used to catching flak from the Southeastern Conference players; most of his NFL clients came out of the league. The once-proud Vols were barely an afterthought by November these days, and he heard about it often.

"This year is going to be different," he said, sliding behind the wheel of his Corvette – a 1963 classic, marina blue with side pipes and a split rear window. The 1963 was the only Corvette of that model generation that had a split rear window. The car used to belong to his father. Billy drove it rarely, but had decided to dust it off for Leroy's commercial shoot in Atlanta. "Jarvis Thompson will be the difference."

"Now that's a *real* car," Mitchell said. "Good old-fashioned American muscle. I can relate to that."

"You wouldn't fit in this one either, Leroy."

Mitchell waved and climbed into his big truck.

"Good luck to Jarvis and all the poor Vols this weekend. We'll take care of business here. See you down the road, brother."

The road never seemed to end for Billy. He'd been logging some serious miles, trying to stay ahead, and he did some of his best work on the move. Wherever he found himself, he was fielding calls from players, their families, team officials, sponsors, physicians. Any one of those calls could turn into an adventure that only Billy could manage, and that's the way he liked it. Negotiating skills went only so far in his business. The personal touch, treating your clients like family, that's what set you apart in the long run.

Billy was still a few steps behind the big management firms and the famous agents who had catered to the superstars for years and were fabulously wealthy. But he was working hard and gaining ground, especially in the NFL.

Pro football had become the center of the sports universe, the national obsession. Agents had more to do, more to worry about, and more to gain. The best ones turned their clients into household names – and in the process often became celebrities themselves.

Billy didn't mind basking in the spotlight from time to time, but he was driven by the competition. It was in his blood.

"I'm just a little guy from Sevierville, Tennessee," he once told his father, "but I want the owners and GMs to know I'm in the game. Eventually I'm going to be one of those super agents, walking with the biggest stars, sitting down with the billionaires. They'll want to hear what I have to say."

With Jarvis Thompson on his team, he was that much closer to his dream.

CHAPTER THREE

The Corvette came to life with a throaty roar, and Billy settled in for the three-hour drive back to Knoxville. As he merged into the northbound lanes of Interstate 75, he could already feel the knot forming in his stomach. It happened every time he drove past the site of the crash. He took a deep breath and thought of his mother.

Anna Beckett was the primary reason he was in this line of work. She was the one who had instilled the competitive spirit, the love of sports, the take-charge attitude in both her sons when they were young. They quickly developed into outstanding athletes.

Their father, Franklin, was a cop in Sevierville who worked a lot of weekend shifts, so in the summer it was up to Anna to ferry them from baseball tournament to tournament all around the Southeast. The teenagers would share some of the driving duties. It was a team effort, and they all relished their time together.

They were heading to Marietta, on the edge of Atlanta, on that fateful day. The area was a hotbed for baseball talent, a place for young players to make a name for themselves. Anna had stopped for gas. John and Billy argued over which one would spell their mother for a bit, give her a few minutes to close her eyes and stretch out. Billy, the oldest, won the argument and took the wheel of the silver Toyota Camry.

A half-hour later, the car was lying on its top, wheels up, in the middle of the median. Billy had been distracted by something John said and had looked at him in the rear-view mirror for just a second, but that second was all it took. He'd barely clipped the rear of a tractor-trailer. The impact sent the Camry veering sharply off the shoulder of the highway and into the grass.

Anna, who had been sitting beside Billy, didn't have her seat belt fastened. She was thrown from the rolling vehicle and lay unconscious at the edge of the pavement. Billy and John were still buckled in, bleeding and disoriented but relatively unscathed as the sirens of approaching emergency vehicles wailed.

They were only five minutes away from the nearest hospital, but it was too late for Anna. She was pronounced dead on arrival.

All these years later, her scream, the sounds of twisting metal, the realization that his mother had been thrown from the car, were still clear in Billy's mind. He drove past the Windy Hill Road exit and glanced over for only a second, then mashed the Corvette's accelerator.

There was plenty left on the day's agenda. The messages on Billy's phone always accumulated quickly, and he wasn't one to let them sit for long.

Rule number one: There had to be constant contact.

"Hi, Rachel," he said. "I'm finished here; everything went great with Leroy and I had a good meeting earlier. How are things at the office?"

"I put together those player packets you wanted," Rachel said. "You can give them a look when you get back to town."

"I'd like the one for Fred Taylor's family sent off as soon as possible. Those Alabama running backs are hard to get a handle on, and this is the perfect week to grab his attention. I'm heading your way now."

The packets were Billy's calling card. They contained his mission statement, outlined potential marketing opportunities, and explained how he would prepare a particular player for the combine and the draft. The agent had to calculate how much time and money to invest in each player. Two weeks of training, with room and board, could run ten thousand dollars or more. If a client dropped in the draft, or if something drastic happened and he fell out of the draft entirely, the agent found himself eating the cost.

There weren't many Jarvis Thompsons waiting out there. Sure first-rounders were like gold and usually got snapped up by the established management firms. The players at the very top of the draft were in a class of their own.

Even with one in hand, Billy couldn't afford to make bad decisions. Those five years in Atlanta had been lucrative, but he was still heavily leveraged. Big house, boat, cars, travel expenses. Material things didn't particularly motivate Billy, but there was a certain image that needed to be maintained. He was betting that his strong connections and instincts would keep his career moving forward, along with his charm. Billy was as driven as his clients, yet he had a way of putting anyone around him at ease.

He liked to think his mother would have been proud.

"Hello, Mark," Billy said as the Corvette eased back into the right lane with that distinctive purr. "Got a few minutes?"

"Anything for you, man," came the reply. "What's up?"

Mark Fletcher was a private investigator and had worked for several NFL teams, including the Falcons. Billy had hired him to look into character issues and legal entanglements with players a few times. He liked Fletcher's style. The man was well connected around the league and had a discreet way of getting to the truth.

He had become a trusted friend, which was a valuable commodity for any sports agent.

"Tell me about Sonny Bradley and his people in New Orleans," Billy said. "I keep hearing they're crossing the line on some of these new players. Do you know anything?"

"Nothing specific," Fletcher said, "but there have been some rumblings lately about illegal contacts and payoffs. There's a guy down there that has his hand in a lot of bad stuff, and he may be involved with Bradley. From what I understand, he wants to get deeper into the sports business, is dangling some carrots, and several of the coaches along the Gulf are starting to bite. That kind of influence trickles down in a hurry."

"What's his name?"

"Frank Romano."

"What does the players union think?"

"They're waiting to see, like always. Bradley could lose his certification if he's not careful, but you know how that goes."

Billy definitely knew. There were hundreds of certified agents out there, and some of them were flagrant rule breakers. Most bent the rules from time to time. *If you ain't cheatin', you ain't tryin'*, the old maxim went. But unless you flaunted the rules *and* were caught red-handed, most people tended to look the other way.

"What's the background on Bradley?" Billy said. "Seems like he just showed up out of nowhere."

"Not many people I've talked to know much about him. He's a New Orleans guy and started building his business in that area. As you're aware, there are enough great athletes down there to fuel a few pro teams. I heard Bradley has around twenty clients at this point, so he's been coming on pretty fast."

Billy had crossed paths with more than a few unscrupulous wannabes along the way and was always on guard. It was easy to make enemies, especially with more and more money on the line, and he wasn't going to be undermined if he could help it.

"Bradley has really put the press on with Jarvis Thompson," he said. "Under the circumstances, I don't understand where it's coming from."

"I thought that kid was in the clear with you. You've earned his trust. Why would anything change?"

"I don't know that it would. I just keep hearing things."

"I wouldn't worry about it too much," Fletcher said. "I assume Jarvis is coming out this year, so he'll be tied up soon. You know what you're doing."

Billy was indeed a student of the game – all the games. He understood the psychology of sports, the power of persuasion, what buttons to push. He could connect with people; it was a gift.

The NFL wasn't the most financially rewarding league for agents – three percent of playing contracts was the maximum commission – but it went much deeper for Billy. He'd been a star quarterback in high school and was already emotionally invested in the football culture, guys laying their bodies on the line day in and day out, playing through pain and sacrificing until they had no more to give. In his mind, it was the noblest of games.

Most of the pros didn't have long to cash in on their careers. And when it was over, there wasn't much else to fall back on. They all needed a good agent to guide them through the journey, put them in the best financial position for life beyond football. They needed a savvy, fiercely loyal advocate like Billy.

"The best protection a man can have" was how one client described him, and he considered that the ultimate compliment. The question was, who protected the agent?

Most often, the agent had to protect himself.

"I think it may be time to have a little talk with Mr. Bradley," Billy said to Fletcher, "just to let him know he's on my radar. I appreciate your help as always, Mark. Let's have a beer soon. My treat, of course."

"Of course," Fletcher said. "Be careful out there. You know how things can turn nasty pretty quick in this business."

Billy laughed.

"And they said it would be all fun and games."

CHAPTER FOUR

The sound of gunfire crackled through the congested neighborhood, one pop and then another. Jarvis scooted to the edge of the window and peered out at the street. Nothing but darkness.

He crouched on the floor again and waited for danger to pass. Fear turned to anger in those minutes, and then, resignation. The Saturday late-night drill had almost become routine in his decrepit little corner of Autumn, Florida.

Across the hall, there were the muffled giggles and groans of a crack whore entertaining another stranger, earning her latest fix, oblivious to her surroundings. The crack whore was his mother. Jarvis was the only other man in the house – hell, the only real man in the family – and he was just a teenager.

He and football would be their salvation. It was all up to him.

"We can't stay here, Jarvis," Tianna, his sister, would say. "Things are only going to get worse. We'll die, one way or another. You know we will. We have to get out."

The words still echoed in his head. The escape was never complete, not even now with the NFL draft – and the potential for freedom it would offer – in sight.

Jarvis rolled over on the bed in his apartment and glanced at his phone, which had been silenced. Another missed call from his mother. That was three already today. Even in her perpetual stupor, Clarise never let up. She was counting the days.

"Crazy woman," Jarvis muttered to himself.

Still feeling the effects of a long practice, he closed his eyes again, and the images continued to stream through his mind. He had tried to suppress them in the years since coming to Knoxville, make a fresh start, but it was useless. At times like this, when he was alone and drifting, they could play like an endless loop, still vivid, never far away.

The burning rage of his parents. The fights. The gunshots. The helplessness.

Life in the projects had almost consumed them all, and it wasn't something a young man could ever forget, even one destined for greatness on the football field.

Jarvis pulled the foam pillow tight around his head, as if that could block it all out. The pillow was one of the few remaining possessions that he had brought from Florida, a small comfort. He couldn't bring himself to toss it in the trash. It was a connection to *her*, the one person he'd never forget.

Tianna was his only sister, one year older. For many years they shared a small, dimly lit room in Autumn. Jarvis would lie on the floor at the foot of her bed most nights, wrapped up in his dirty blankets with his head resting on that pillow. They would talk for hours, try to make sense of their lives while all hell was breaking loose around them – the brazen drug dealers; the strange noises just outside open windows on warm Florida nights; the debauchery of their mother; the absence of their father and older brother.

"We can't stay here." But they did, night after terrible night.

Jarvis could have moved in with his high school coach, the only man resembling a father figure in his life. The coach's home was a frequent refuge. But there was no way Jarvis would leave Tianna to face the horrors alone.

Their brother, Dante, might have been a buffer once. But he was almost a decade older and long gone by the time the kids were teens. Like their father, he had become a transient, moving from place to place, hoping to sell more drugs than he consumed just to get by.

Jarvis had to stay for Tianna. He often told her he was playing football for *them*, just the two of them. It was their one glimmer of hope, and if he made it all the way to the NFL, he promised to take her with him. Those dreams carried the teenagers through the worst of times.

Football was the simple part. Jarvis was a man among boys on the field but still had to fight for respect. Early on, he was involved in many a skirmish with his high school teammates, always being tested and measured, until he simply became too much to handle.

Even after being voted a team captain as a sophomore, some could never accept him. The toughest kids from the projects were jealous that he was destined for a future they would never have. He had a way out.

One day early in his sophomore season, Jarvis was walking toward home behind three teammates when they suddenly stopped and formed a wall in front of him.

"So you're a captain already?" one boy said. He pulled a knife from his backpack. "You think you're better than us cause you're going to college, don't you? I got news for you, bro. You ain't."

Jarvis stopped and glared at the linebacker, a senior who was a notorious troublemaker feared by most on the team. At sixteen, Jarvis had grown used to thugs and bullies. He was unafraid.

"We're the same once we're off the field," Jarvis said to the linebacker. "We all have to find a way to get by, every day." He then dropped his backpack at his feet. "If you want to keep getting by, put the knife up and walk away while you can. Otherwise, I'll leave you here in pieces."

The other teammates backed away from the confrontation, and the linebacker quickly followed. The story made the rounds at school the next day, another chapter in the growing legend of Jarvis Thompson. He was never directly challenged again.

He would go on to lead his team to two state championships before heading off to Tennessee. He had survived – and made his hometown proud in the process.

Tianna, tragically, didn't wait to join Jarvis on his climb to the pros.

She married a soldier at eighteen and moved to Texas to start a new life. *"We have to get out."* The violence followed her. Her husband, an older man who had served two tours in Iraq, told police he came home one night and she was gone. He had a history of mental illness and abuse, and they suspected he had murdered her, but there was never a trace. Just another girl from the ghetto gone missing.

Months later they found the man slumped over the wheel of his pickup truck, dead from a self-inflicted gunshot wound. No notes, no confessions.

Tianna's disappearance still weighed heavily on Jarvis. He hadn't been able to save her, to fulfill his promise, and he knew that failure would haunt him for the rest of his life.

But it also had become a motivating force as his college days wound down. Jarvis was playing for *her* now. The glory was still there for the taking, and he knew she was watching. He *had* to deliver.

Suddenly, Jarvis was startled out of semi-consciousness. He felt a hand on his shoulder.

"Hey, you all right?" His roommate, Brett, was shaking him awake. "I could hear you moaning from the kitchen. Man, your shirt is soaking wet. More of those bad dreams?"

Jarvis took a deep breath and tried to regain his bearing as he sat up in bed. Finally, an uneasy smile. The past was back in its place.

"It's nothing," he said. "I need to call home. Give me a couple minutes and we'll go."

CHAPTER FIVE

The call to his mother went immediately to voicemail. Jarvis flipped on the television and began to pull tight the laces of his sneakers. The banter on ESPN had turned to college football. The studio host directed his attention to Knoxville and a reporter on site. "Is there any chance that the Alabama train gets derailed at Neyland Stadium this weekend?" he asked. "Could this be a trap game for the nation's top-ranked team?"

"We've been saying that about this series for more than a decade," the reporter said. "It used to be a battle – I mean, Peyton Manning never lost to Alabama – but that was a long time ago. Now it's nothing more than a trap game. The recent history is all in the Tide's favor, and I don't see Tennessee hanging around in this one for long either, unless they can get the ball to Jarvis Thompson early and often."

"He's having another great year. I'd hate to see where the Vols would be without him."

"They'd better enjoy him while they can. I'm pretty sure we'll see him playing on Sundays next fall."

Jarvis glanced at the screen and smiled to himself. Even with an also-ran team, he was part of the national conversation.

The receiver stood and picked up a football from the foot of his bed. He quietly counted his blessings, again. Win or lose, he was moving forward. There was no reason to look back. He now had real teammates, real friends, a real future.

It could all have gone south at any moment, of course, if not for Billy. Fate and the football gods had somehow brought them together. "Dumb luck," the agent liked to call it.

Jarvis's brother, Dante, and Billy's brother, John, were baseball teammates for a year at Florida State. Jarvis would find rides over from Autumn on the weekends to hang out and watch the Seminoles play. Billy, who would drive down from Knoxville every chance he got, met him one day at the ballpark and was intrigued.

At such a tender age, Jarvis had manners and an engaging air about him, and he always carried a football to the baseball games. In fact, he carried one everywhere he went.

"Coach says to keep one close," he'd say. "Learn to love that leather. Treat it like your best friend and it'll always be good to you."

Before long, Billy learned that the boy and his family were struggling just to stay afloat, how Jarvis's father had drifted away leaving his dysfunctional mother to manage three children, how the baby of the family was left to practically raise himself.

Later, when he was working in Atlanta, Billy called Jarvis regularly to check up on him. He liked the boy, and it seemed like a natural thing to do, the right thing to do.

By the time Jarvis reached high school, he was a man in many ways, and already a well-known football prospect in Florida – bigger, stronger and faster than other receivers at the elite summer camps. He had other attributes, too: a magnetic personality and a powerful will to win. The mighty in-state programs at Florida State, Florida and Miami all had their sights set on him.

But Tennessee had the inside track to signing him, even though its coaches couldn't have known at the time.

"We're going to team up one day," Billy told Jarvis when he made the decision to become a sports agent. "You're going to be the best receiver in football, and I'm going to be driving your bandwagon all the way to the Super Bowl."

Once Billy returned to Knoxville, he continued to focus on cultivating one of the NFL's top talents. Jarvis may have come into his orbit in a roundabout way, but as time went on, there became little doubt that they needed each other.

As with many things in Jarvis's life, the decisive move to Knoxville was born out of tragedy.

He had been seeing Denise Rollins, a feisty girl from school who wasn't afraid of all the things she had heard about the Thompson family. They had become especially close, helping to fill the emotional void for Jarvis when his sister moved away. Denise was an honors student from a good family, a positive influence. They planned to attend college together, to see where things might lead.

One night she was leaving Jarvis's house when three shots rang out. Jarvis raced outside and found her in the yard, gasping and bleeding heavily. She died in his arms. The boys who killed her were drug-dealing gang bangers. They mistook her for another girl, but she was still dead.

If not for Billy, who drove all night from Tennessee to reach him, Jarvis might have thrown away his future that night. He wanted revenge, and he might very well have either been killed or sent to prison. But Billy kept him on the phone, kept him calm until he could get there.

Looking back, that was a crossroads in both of their lives. The tragedy cemented an unbreakable bond. Billy was the one who had always believed in the kid, kept him focused, and ultimately led him out of the projects.

Jarvis tried to placate his mother on occasion, but deep down, he knew his future rested with Billy. Because Billy cared, he genuinely cared about Jarvis as a person, and Jarvis knew it.

CHAPTER SIX

Billy had friends in the union offices, and it didn't take the agent long to come up with a cell number for Sonny Bradley. This would be their first real conversation.

They had met two or three years ago, just briefly at a popular watering hole in Indianapolis. It was the end of another long day at the player combine, the infamous meat market that essentially serves as the NFL's annual trade show. Players, coaches, scouts, executives, agents and reporters are thrown together in face-to-face situations, and the results help determine a player's draft status.

It didn't take much to change things for a player. Questions about character, a slow time in the forty, a low Wonderlic Test score – almost anything could cost a player, and his agent, significant amounts of money. The perceptions of total strangers mattered.

There was no better chance than combine week for charmers like Billy to spin and promote their clients to anyone willing to listen. Especially after a few drinks. A big group had gathered at the bar that night. An acquaintance of Billy's introduced Bradley as an attorney from

Slidell, Louisiana, who was a newcomer to the business. Maybe he called him a "consultant." They shook hands.

That was about all Billy could remember as the phone rang in New Orleans.

"Hello, Sonny," he said. "Billy Beckett here."

There was a long pause, then a Cajun chuckle.

"You mean, *the* Billy Beckett?" Bradley said. "Well, long time no see, man. What can I do for you?"

"I've been hearing your name a lot lately and just wanted you to know I was thinking about you."

"Really? I'm flattered."

"Don't be," Billy said. "Jarvis Thompson tells me you – or your representatives – paid his mother a visit down in Florida last week, and she's suddenly all hot and bothered again about what he's going to do, even though it's been obvious for a while. That's not playing nice."

"C'mon, Billy, you know it's just part of the game. We're not playing outside the lines here. Besides, I like Clarise. Don't you?"

Bradley sounded like a real agent. A little humor, a little bob and weave to disguise ulterior motives. He had learned his lessons well.

"She's a drunken witch, and everybody knows it," Billy said. "Jarvis knows it, too. He won't be changing his mind just because his mother is looking for a payoff."

Bradley laughed. "I thought the boy still loved his mother."

"He does, as much as a son can love a mother who has always put herself before him, but he's seen more than enough to know what she's about. And I think he has a pretty good idea of what you're about. This kid isn't going to sign with you, so you might as well move on. I'm sure you've got plenty more shady deals in the works."

"You're starting to hurt my feelings, Billy. Sounds like you're Jarvis's daddy now, too, even though you're a little young for that. I don't suppose you're bending any rules up there in Tennessee. Sounds to me like you're awfully close to the situation. Maybe too close. Some people might be interested in that."

Trying to turn the tables. Another tactic.

"Maybe you didn't know I was his guardian for a while," Billy said, "and I care a hell of a lot more about Jarvis than his daddy ever did. I'm not going to put him in a bad position. That's where we're different. From what I hear, you guys down there are willing to do about anything to lock up these young players who don't know any better, and they're going to regret it down the road."

"I don't know where you get that," Bradley said. "We're just doing our due diligence and trying to make a living. Just like you."

Billy had heard enough, but he couldn't let the conversation die just yet. He wanted to know more about Bradley's alleged boss.

"Tell me about Frank Romano," he said. "Sounds like a dangerous guy. Word is that he's pulling your strings."

"Don't even know him, only what I've read. You probably know more about Frank Romano than I do."

"How's that?"

"You really should mind your own business, Billy. Getting into mine isn't a good idea."

"Maybe I need to come down to New Orleans so we can look each other in the eye. I haven't been to the Big Easy in a while. Might be fun."

"I wouldn't advise it," Bradley said. "I'd love to see you, of course, but there's no need to stir up a bunch of trouble for nothing. It wouldn't take much for a Tennessee boy like you to get into some pretty deep shit here."

"Ah, a threat," Billy said. "I love it. Let me give you a little advice: don't push this. The season is getting late, and I'm going to make sure it ends like it's supposed to. My guys are my guys, and rest assured, Jarvis Thompson is my guy."

"Whatever you say, man. I gotta go. Call any time, and good luck with your guy."

Billy put down the phone and took a couple of deep breaths as he worked the Corvette through traffic. His hands were trembling slightly and he could feel his pulse pounding at his temples.

Bastard, he thought to himself. *This isn't over. Not even close.*

CHAPTER SEVEN

"**W**ell, it's nice to see you again."

Rachel sounded agitated when Billy walked into his Knoxville office just before five o'clock. The pile of paperwork had grown in his absence, and the calls kept streaming in.

Billy never knew how his girlfriend would handle the rush of business on a given day, especially when he hadn't been around to stroke her ego. His office manager was gone, too, so he knew it had been a long day for Rachel.

"You look awesome today, girl," Billy said, leaning in for a kiss. The comment was lost on the statuesque brunette, who rarely had a bad day when it came to looks. She moved quickly past him.

It was no secret that Rachel King wasn't cut out for secretarial work. She grew up in privilege in the low country of South Carolina and had been a star athlete in college. She'd been a star pretty much all her life, in fact. Naturally, she was expecting a more glamorous lifestyle when she agreed to leave a promising real-estate gig in Atlanta and move in with an upstart sports agent.

Billy probably expected the lifestyle to be a little more glamorous, too, but he'd quickly learned that the business had plenty of mundane moments.

"The packet you wanted is on your desk," Rachel said. "Candace will be back in the office tomorrow, which is good for all of us. You know I'm better out in the field."

"You're definitely a player, but the job is what it is. Some days I need you to be a team player."

"I'm going home and soak in the spa for a while. Will you be joining me?"

"I have a few more calls to make," Billy said. "Give me two hours and I'll give you the rest of the night."

"That's mighty big of you. How about bringing some food. I'd vote for Italian, and maybe a bottle of that Barolo we had a while back. That'd be a good start."

"Would it guarantee a good finish?"

Rachel managed a smug smile and turned to leave.

"Yes?" Billy said.

"Maybe."

The couple had been living together off and on for a while now, and it was quite the roller coaster ride. The highs were still exhilarating, but they didn't come along as often anymore. The lows could be downright frigid.

Sometimes it was hard to remember that first meeting, the electricity they both felt. Cold November night in Atlanta. Hospitality suite at a Falcons game. Two strangers talking in a quiet corner, getting warmer by the minute.

Billy was a corporate lawyer on the rise, tall and ruggedly handsome with curly dark hair and a perpetually unshaven face. He looked like an athlete, and that was the way he carried himself.

Rachel had been an all-conference volleyball player at the University of Georgia, a poster girl for the sport who once had Olympic aspirations. Instead, she moved on with life and was making good use of her business degree and other assets with a trendy real-estate firm in Westside. The perks of her job were growing by the day when Billy came along and steered her in an exciting new direction.

He was seven years older and had a different aura about him. They laughed and the conversation was easy.

"What's a nice girl like you doing watching a sorry team like this?" was how it all began. They didn't watch much more of the game.

Before long, they were going out regularly, then sharing a downtown apartment. There was certainly chemistry, and the sex was powerful, different than any-thing Billy had ever experienced. He'd never been at the pleasure of such an uninhibited woman.

"Are you sure you're just twenty-four?" he said the first time Rachel cast her spell. "Seems like you've learned an awful lot about men."

"Men are simple creatures," she replied.

That much hadn't changed, except the simple crea-ture of the house didn't spend as much time doting on her these days. Growing the business had proved to be a daunting challenge, more work than play on every front. Billy was often gone or distracted, and Rachel was left to entertain herself. She'd sometimes go to great lengths to do so.

More and more, she was making the five-hour drive home to Charleston to visit with friends and family. The lure of the sun, sand and surf kept pulling her back.

This weekend would be different. With the top-ranked Crimson Tide in town, the schedule had been cleared and Rachel and Billy would jump on his houseboat and be part of the Vol Navy that ruled the water outside the stadium. Hopefully Jarvis Thompson would have a huge game, raise his draft stock another notch, and the home team would somehow end this awful losing streak.

"I'll see you at home," Rachel said on her way out the door.

Billy turned to admire that fabulous form and flashed a smile. "Can't wait."

CHAPTER EIGHT

The stage was set for another of those magical inter-
ludes as Billy walked in from the garage with his
arms full of food and drink.

Candlelight filled the big house with a warm glow.
Vanilla incense sweetened the air, and a reggae beat
pulsed down from the rafters. Bob Marley always had a
way of enhancing the mood.

Rachel was nowhere to be seen, so Billy quickly
opened the bottle of Barolo, grabbed a couple of glasses
from the bar and made his way upstairs. Dinner could
wait.

The fireplace in the master suite flickered and steam
was rising from the freshly filled spa that overlooked the
river at the end of the corridor. Through the frosted glass
of the bathroom door, Billy could see Rachel standing at
the vanity. She was admiring herself in the mirror, and
for good reason.

He poured the wine and noticed he was breathing
a little heavy. She wasn't even in the room, yet just the
thought of her aroused him.

Billy was a striking man, and the many hours in the
gym showed as he peeled off his clothes. He turned on

the spa jets and eased himself into the hot water, tilting his head back against a long cushion.

"Let me know if there's anything I can do to help," he said loud enough for her to hear.

The bathroom door opened and Rachel glided out in all her splendor, wearing a sheer pearl cover-up that left just enough to the imagination. Almost as tall as Billy, with olive skin and piercing hazel eyes, she was a stunning beauty.

"You're early," she said.

"Looks like I'm right on time. Have I mentioned lately how smoking hot you are? You could be working for Victoria's Secret."

She smiled and stopped to offer a runway pose. "Had you forgotten?"

"If I had, you just reminded me." Billy stretched out his hand. "Come closer."

"Seems like it's been a long time," he said. "Too long."

"Whose fault is that?"

"I'll take the blame. But all the work is paying off. We're on our way, baby."

Rachel put a forefinger to his lips. "Enough talk about work," she said.

Sweeping her dark hair from her face, she rubbed her cheek against his and breathed lustily into his ear. *Is This Love* cranked from the speakers above and all was right in Billy's world.

His relationships with women had always been temporary. He'd run a gauntlet of them, never sticking with one for long. In the end, they always seemed to turn out to be a distraction he didn't need.

Rachel was different from the start.

She was at ease in any setting, work or play. Her luscious curves tended to catch the attention of prospective clients long before Billy's business savvy did, especially when she flashed that beautiful smile and turned on the Southern charm.

She was an asset, at least in his mind. Most everyone close to Billy told him she was trouble waiting to happen.

***

They climbed out of the tub, toweled each other off, and made their way to the bedroom. Thirty minutes later, Billy rolled over in the sheets and exhaled deeply. It wasn't quite a sigh of relief, but something close.

"You're amazing," he said. "Absolutely amazing."

Rachel sat up and reached for her robe. "What did you expect? I hope I didn't take your appetite. How about some dinner and another glass of wine?"

"Sure, but I don't think it'll compare to dessert."

Rachel leaned over and held his face with both hands, looking deeply into his big, brown eyes.

"I've missed you and your body," she said. "Especially your body."

"I could tell, and I'm ready to get reacquainted further. Let's see if we can make up for lost time this weekend. Fall and football and all those other f-words. Feeling free in Tennessee."

"You're really good with f-words," Rachel said. "Maybe your f-ing team will even win. Might as well dream big while you're at it."

"I'm afraid my Vols are a long shot at best, but hopefully Jarvis will do his thing. This is a huge game for him on the national stage, and I expect him to rise to the occasion. The kid is going to open some lucrative doors for us."

Billy smiled contently.

"But first things first," he said. "Let's eat, and then I'd like another taste of that dessert."

CHAPTER NINE

The sea breezes were beginning to freshen again after a long, hot summer on the Gulf of Mexico.

Frank Romano stood on the bow of his cruiser and looked out over the blue-green water as the speedboat approached just south of Grand Isle. Romano was rarely present for these clandestine deliveries in the barrier islands, but he wanted to be seen and heard on this day.

The white boat with the canary yellow racing stripes slowed and the two men aboard got to their feet and prepared to make contact. They had the typical look of drug runners in the area – tan and grim-faced, anxious to unload their cargo and head back toward open water. Their boat bobbed in the light chop as the engine idled with a low growl.

"Hola," Romano said, leaning on the rail. "How's the fishing today?"

"Pretty good," the driver said. "A big catch for you."

They tied off and the other man began pulling out small brown packages in shrink-wrap, dozens of them, and hurriedly tossed them onto the deck of the cruiser. The three bodyguards with Romano collected them, stacked them in the hold and threw a tarp over the pile. In less than ten minutes, the deal was done.

"That's all," the driver said as he reeled in his ropes. "See you next time."

"Just one more thing," Romano said. "Tell your boss that the last shipment fell short. Way short. Didn't he think I'd notice?"

"I just bring what they give me. If there are problems, you have to take it up with the boss."

Romano flashed a wicked smile. "There *are* problems. And since I don't see your boss, I'm going to take it up with you and your friend."

The guard standing to the right of the big man raised a submachine gun and leveled it at the passenger on the speedboat. The man froze.

"Tell your boss I'm personally offended," Romano said. "And if it happens again, he won't even get his boat back."

The sound of the burst from the Uzi rolled like a wave across the water's surface. The passenger reeled backwards, coming to rest in a bloody heap at the rear of the boat. The driver looked up in horror, red spatter dotting his face, and gunned the engine. Soon he was a speck on the horizon.

Romano turned and calmly walked into the cabin.

"Let's get back to shore," he said. "It's a damned shame we have to do business like this sometimes. Things used to be more civilized."

***

It was hard to remember, but there once was a time when Romano was kept under wraps, for fear of what he might become.

From the beginning, his mother had tried to shelter him. She'd even given him her maiden name, which wouldn't raise so many red flags along the coast. She tried to occupy his mind with productive tasks, tried to keep him away from the riff-raff that was always coming around.

But nothing she did mattered for long.

Unfortunately, young Frankie was his father's boy. He had that volatile nature, that same cruel streak, and he was headed for a life of crime.

By the time Romano was old enough to vote – not that he ever considered it – he was already bold, brash, and dangerous. The mob mentality was ingrained in him and he reveled in the sense of entitlement. He idolized his father, who was in control of every situation, almost to the end.

As he approached forty, delusions of grandeur had long since taken hold. Romano's ego and growing territory needed constant feeding. A Louisiana newspaper had recently referred to him as "the scourge of New Orleans," and as the body count grew, there was no question that Frank Romano was a ruthless man indeed.

At the same time, he was a shadowy figure with few direct lines of access, cunning enough to keep the authorities at bay with payoffs and sheer guile. He had become an underground legend in a city notorious for its corruption and blatantly lawless ways. Some said he was untouchable.

"Don't ever feel like you're bulletproof," his father used to warn him, "because someone out there will always want to take you down. You just can't let them get close enough to do it."

Romano's father, Anthony Matranga, would proudly leave the family business in the capable hands of his son when the feds finally carted him off to prison. And now, with his own being groomed for greatness, Frank Romano planned to carry on the tradition.

***

"I'm sorry you had to witness that," Frank said as he sat across from the young man with shoulder-length brown hair and a wispy beard.

Paul Romano had been casually picking a guitar in the cabin, emotionally detached, it seemed, from the mayhem that had just occurred on deck. He looked strangely out of place with this dark-haired gang of mobsters, but his eyes revealed that he belonged. They were as cold and calculating as his father's.

"Take us in," Frank said.

Paul carefully laid the Taylor guitar back in its case and moved behind the wheel of the cruiser. The engine fired. The other men braced themselves to keep watch on the short ride back to Grand Isle.

"So this was my welcome home?" Paul said. "Was it really necessary to bring me out here on a drug deal and kill some poor fool right in front of me? Was that supposed to impress me?"

"You just need to be aware. It's a dangerous business full of dangerous people, and sometimes you have to send a message. You have to get your business partners' full attention. I guarantee you, there will be no more shortages. We'll have no more problems with those gentlemen. Understand?"

Paul simply nodded and turned his gaze to the water.

"Have you done any more with our little project in Tennessee?" his father said. "It's time to move."

"I'm going up there this weekend and try to put things in motion. Tommy and Gene are already there. I think everything will fall into place, one way or another."

"Will the girl help us?"

"I think so. She probably won't know she's doing it, but she likes me. We got to be pretty good friends in Charleston."

"And that's all?"

"She's a free spirit. She's fun, not to mention extremely easy on the eyes. I'd like to get her down here and show her around some day."

"I don't think her boyfriend would like that."

"Maybe he could come, too," Paul said with a grin. "You'd enjoy that, wouldn't you?"

The men sat quietly for several minutes as the boat made its way along the perimeter of the nature preserve. They had spent many afternoons in the waters around the barrier islands, where Louisianans went to relax and simply enjoy the tranquility of the Gulf.

"I don't want any problems," Romano said. "What if the player doesn't cooperate?"

"I believe he will. We can play it either way."

"Your grandfather deserves to have this done right. He'd be proud of you taking the initiative on a job like this. I wasn't sure we'd ever get you back."

"Me either. Strange how things work out sometimes."

Several brown pelicans glided by in formation, scanning the waves for their next meal. The breeze flowed through Paul's hair as he drove.

"I'm looking forward to the weekend," he said. "A little shock and awe is always good for the soul."

CHAPTER TEN

The men were hunkered down in a cheap motel on the edge of town, waiting for instructions. There was a growing sense of unease in the room.

"This has a bad feel to it. Sending us here, to Knoxville, Tennessee, of all places? Watching a college football player? What the hell is *that* about?"

Gene Casey sat on the edge of the bed cleaning a semi-automatic pistol, his eyes darting constantly as he spoke. He was ex-Army, an infantryman, thin with stringy reddish hair and a dark countenance that caused most strangers to steer clear. Even his few friends called him "Mean Gene."

Across from him, on the other double bed, Tommy Blanchard looked up from his carton of Chinese takeout and shrugged his shoulders. The two worked together often, and he took his partner's doom and gloom in stride.

"We do what we're told," Tommy said. "No sense getting worked up about it."

"I don't like being told anything by kids. I gave that up when I left Afghanistan. What's the plan here anyway? We don't usually go anywhere without knowing what we're doing."

"This is coming from the boss, not the kid, so you know there's a plan. Paul will be here soon, though, and I guess we'll find out what it's all about. Relax."

Gene reached over and laid his weapon on the bedside table between them. The Smith & Wesson M&P 9mm was his favorite handgun, and he rarely let it get out of arm's reach for more than a moment. Old habit.

"I don't trust Paul," he said. "I'm not sure why the boss does either. He's an amateur, hasn't proven anything. That can be dangerous."

"But he's family. Big Frank expects him to take over the business one day, just like he did for his father."

"Personally, I don't see it. I don't think Junior has the stones for this kind of work. Hell, wasn't he playing in a rock-n-roll band or something not long ago? Seriously? Hard to go from that to this."

Gene got up and began to pace. His stint in the Army had molded him into a proficient killer, but it also had left him anxious.

He parted the curtains and looked out the small window. There was a narrow view of the back parking lot, with the black SUV sitting beside the motel dumpsters. He could see cars whizzing down Interstate 40 in the distance.

"You remember how to get back to the high-rent district?" he said.

"Same way we went last time. I remember."

"You know I had a bead on both of them. Could have killed him. Could have killed them both. Easy."

"We're not here for a hit, unless something changes," Tommy said. "That was just a reconnaissance mission.

You remember those, right? Maybe our football player ends up like his old man. Maybe not."

"Hard to believe he's even part of the same family. Gonna be a big star in the pros, if he makes it that far. I don't watch football, but that's what everybody says."

"What about his brother? He sounded more like Daddy's boy. Have you heard anything more about him lately?"

"Not since he was down in New Orleans asking questions. I'm not real worried about him. If he's a piece of garbage like Charles, he won't be around long anyway. He'll be flushed away."

There was a tap at the door, and within seconds Gene had the gun back in his hand and was staring out the peephole.

"Housekeeping."

The maid tapped again and Gene suddenly smiled. "Want to have some fun while we're killing time?"

"What do you have in mind?" Tommy said.

Gene held up a finger and slid the security chain off its track and opened the door. A plump Hispanic woman who looked to be in her early thirties smiled at him. Her uniform badge said her name was Maria.

"Would you like service?" she said.

"We certainly would. Come in."

The maid began to grab supplies from her cart as Gene held the door and flashed a sinister nod to his partner. Tommy put his food aside and shook his head.

Maria walked in dutifully with towels in her arms, and Gene slid the chain back on the door. She stopped with a wary look on her face, and then gasped when she saw the gun in his hand.

"We'd like the full service. Dos," Gene said. "We'll pay extra, of course."

Tommy moved close to the maid and waved a few twenties in her face. She dropped the towels on the floor and took a deep breath as Gene walked up behind her and began to unbutton her blouse.

"You are bad men," she said.

"Bad men with money," Tommy said. "Understand?"

"Give it to me." Maria took the cash and smiled. "And put down the gun."

CHAPTER ELEVEN

The final shots were squeezed off in short order.

Pop, pop, pop.

The silhouette showed three lethal hits – two in the head and another right through the heart.

Billy stepped back from the stall and lowered his weapon with a sly smile. The shooting range owner, a gray-haired woman wearing a UT baseball cap, reeled in the target and nodded approvingly. She reached over with a friendly pat to Billy's shoulder as they both pulled off their earmuffs.

"Haven't lost the touch, sugar," she said. "A chip off the old block. How's your father, anyway? He hasn't been out here in a while."

"Don't see him much myself. You know how it is with cops, Marti. Crime never rests, not even in Sevierville. Dad's covered up behind a desk most of the time now. Guess that's what happens when you get to be chief – farther from the action but responsible for all of it. Most days I think he'd rather be back on the streets, or out here target shooting."

"Tell him we miss him. There aren't many guys left who have been members here since I opened. Hell, I remember you and your brother hanging around this place for hours as kids, when you weren't playing ball. John was pretty good with a gun, but your dad turned you into a champ. And now look at you. How's the sports agent business these days anyway?"

"It's getting better, knock on wood."

"Our Vols still aren't much to speak of, and I hate it, especially with Alabama coming to town," Marti said, turning her gaze back toward the big man with the braids, who was standing at a distance with earplugs draped around his neck. "But it's not Jarvis's fault."

Billy waved the receiver over. "Marti here would like to order up a Tennessee victory Saturday. Would you mind?"

"I'll do my best," Jarvis said with a smile. "Just for her… and a couple million others in this state."

Marti chuckled and offered another pat for both men. "Y'all have fun. I'll be watching."

"You better be," Billy said, pulling a loaded magazine from his pocket. He changed it out before placing the black handgun back on the ledge in front of them.

"It's your turn now," he said to Jarvis.

Jarvis was hesitant. "I don't know, Billy. Really, I just came to watch. Needed to get away from all the Knoxville hype for a couple hours."

"I thought you liked hype."

"I do, but I've had enough this week. I'm just ready to play."

"Sounds like the best receiver in the country has some butterflies."

"Always. But don't tell anybody."

"Right now is a good time to work out some stress on those targets."

"Guns don't lower stress for me," Jarvis said. "The sound reminds me of growing up in the projects. And all these black targets make me nervous."

"I thought you said you used to be one."

"Still am."

The men shared a laugh. Jarvis relented and stepped into the firing stall. He took a deep breath, spread his stance, gripped the pistol with both hands and slowly raised his long arms until they were level with the target.

Pop. Pop. Pop. Three bullet holes above the neck.

"I thought you said you weren't good with guns," Billy said.

"I said I didn't like guns, but I learned how to use them."

Billy was impressed as Jarvis emptied the magazine and turned to walk away.

"Pretty good shooting," Billy said. "You know that may come in handy some day. You need to be able to protect yourself. We all do."

Jarvis stopped and looked Billy in the eye. Suddenly, he was dead serious.

"Is that why you brought me here? Let me tell you something. I've always tried to protect myself and the people around me. But I couldn't protect them all, whether I had a gun or not. I've seen enough dying. You know that."

"Easy now. I'm just concerned about some of the people still in your life. It starts with your mother."

"What about her?"

"I think getting involved with Sonny Bradley and those guys in New Orleans is a huge mistake. They're trouble. She seems more interested in getting a cut of the action than doing what's best for you."

"I really don't want her up here this weekend," Jarvis said. "It's a distraction I don't need. At the same time, she's my mother whether I like it or not. I feel like I should try to make her life better if I can."

"I appreciate what you're saying. I just don't want you to get sucked into something that's not of your own making." Billy smiled and punched Jarvis playfully on the shoulder. "You're a great kid, and a hell of a football player. Show everybody on Saturday."

"That's the plan," Jarvis said as his agent put his ear-muffs back on and walked back into the stall.

CHAPTER TWELVE

The game-day setting in Knoxville was unique in the football world, with the dozens of vessels of all shapes and sizes that made up the Vol Navy squeezed together in one massive flotilla along the north bank of the Tennessee River. It was a short walk across Neyland Drive to the heart of the action.

Some of the UT legends, like Peyton Manning and Jason Witten, used to come down and mingle after games. Those were glorious times indeed.

Billy circled the developing scene in his party boat, a sparkling white sixty-footer with *Agent Orange* painted in a flashy font across the back. The boat was the kind of craft built for the long haul – inboard-outboard drive, spacious sundeck on top, two staterooms and all the amenities down below – and wasn't bad in the short run either.

After Billy acquired it in a sweet deal with Rachel's father a couple of years ago, it didn't take long to figure out that a comfortable thirty-minute ride by water sure beat sitting in his Escalade in the throes of game-day traffic. Now it was a ritual.

Today there were Alabama fans on the river, too, and they were easy to spot. They made sure of that with their little red flags flapping in the breeze.

"I'm already tired of seeing that damn A," Billy said as he scanned the floating neighborhood for a place to set up shop.

He'd been coming to these games for as long as he could remember, though not in such grand style. His father was a season-ticket holder and they would make the twenty-five-mile drive from Sevierville with his brother, John, year after year. They'd grab a burger down on the Strip, line the Vol Walk to Neyland Stadium, visit the Rock, soak up the rich tradition all along the way. Most of the time the Vols won and they went home happy.

Alabama week always had a special vibe. Fans felt it as soon as they rolled into town.

Franklin Beckett still talked to Billy about his memories of doing battle with Bear Bryant's teams. He'd speak of sitting behind the end zone and watching the old coach in the checkered houndstooth hat lean on the goalpost during warm-ups, directly in the eye of the storm with his players moving crisply all around him. The UT fans would yell to try to get the Bear's attention, but the living legend never seemed to notice.

His teams would then go out and pound the ball up and down the field, like an army unleashed.

The Crimson Tide was always tough to beat, and today would be no different, even with Jarvis Thompson wearing the orange. The Vols were a two-touchdown underdog at home.

Billy eased the houseboat into the mix and found a spot to tie off. "Feels like a lucky day," he said to Rachel.

The Vol Navy was massing along the shore, for better or worse, and he knew many of the regulars. A steady stream of them would cross his deck over the next several hours.

There was a special camaraderie here, forged by the relentless flow of the river and decades of sharing the travails on the football field across the street. Sadly, there had been a lot more bad times than good in recent years. The national championship was a distant memory now, and winning seasons were getting hard to come by. Morale was drifting, even if the tailgating, or sailgating, was as fine as ever.

"So you're feeling lucky?" Rachel said. "Maybe that's a good sign."

"I'm feeling *sort of* lucky," Billy said. "It'll probably last until we get to the stadium and see those crimson helmets, so let me enjoy it while I can."

Rachel had gotten up early that morning and was already in the spirit of things. Wearing a tight orange top with *Vol-uptuous* splashed seductively in white sequins across the front, she was working on her second tequila sunrise as she surveyed the festivities.

"Cool scene," she said. "Too bad the team isn't as good as the party."

"Used to be," Billy said. "A lot of people have already forgotten the championship years. Now it seems like we're just gluttons for punishment."

Rachel laughed. "Or just gluttons in general."

The text messages had been dinging in all morning. Billy's clients, even the basketball and baseball players, weren't going to miss an opportunity to dish out some grief in advance on game day.

His phone rang again. It was Darius Stevens, the Kansas City Chiefs safety. Billy had been waiting for that one; Stevens was an Alabama grad and never failed to call and place a little wager on the Tide.

"I'll give you a touchdown," he said.

"Give me two and I'll take it," Billy said. "For a hundred bucks."

They settled on twelve points and the agent turned to some quick business.

"I hear Jamal Avery may not be able to go tomorrow," he said. "That's a great opportunity for you to get into the lineup and really show your stuff. Play well and they may not be able to get you out. We'll be in a strong position at the end of the season."

Most of Billy's clients could stand to improve their bargaining position. It wasn't a star-studded group with lots of guaranteed money in their contracts. In fact, only about half were currently starters on their teams, and in the NFL – where players can be cut in the blink of an eye – the work was already tenuous enough.

Billy turned on the satellite TV, sat back on the couch and popped the top on a cold Heineken.

There was another call, and this one he didn't want to take. The 850 area code was the Florida panhandle. He knew it was Jarvis's mother, probably with a new cell number, and that was always bad news.

CHAPTER THIRTEEN

Clarise Thompson had been blessed and cursed. Blessed to have a son like Jarvis, who was strong enough to overcome all odds, and cursed by most everything else in her wretched life.

The prospects of her boy becoming a shining star in the NFL had put the whole mess in a new perspective as he prepared to make the jump. Jarvis was the family's savior, or at least Clarise's.

Just hearing that voice again made Billy's temperature rise.

"Hello, Billy," she said. "I was just checking to make sure everything is all right up there. Is Jarvis ready to play? What time is the game?"

The fact she didn't know when the biggest game of the season started came as no surprise to Billy. He didn't expect much from a pathetic alcoholic whose main concern always was the next drink, or the next hit from a crack pipe. She was alone now, and her addictions had only gotten worse in the years since Jarvis left home. Billy was surprised she even knew what day it was.

"It's at three-thirty, Clarise, and I'm guessing Jarvis is ready to play. I don't usually talk to him on the morning of games. I'm sure I'll see him later. Is there anything else?"

"No, just tell him I called." And with that she was gone.

She and Billy had never agreed on much of anything when it came to her youngest son. Knowing she had been pushing Jarvis to sign with another agent, right here at the end of his college career, after all Billy had done for the kid, was just a new, contentious chapter in the making.

There was certainly plenty of money at stake all around. The receiver's four-year rookie contract and a hefty signing bonus could top thirty million dollars, not to mention the potential endorsement revenue. And the income would only grow as Jarvis's immense talent and personality were put on full display.

Billy knew Sonny Bradley had been in Autumn just a week ago to make his latest pitch to Clarise and was sure a nice payoff had been promised if she could pry her son away. Jarvis had also mentioned that Bradley arrived with flowers, chocolates and a big bottle of Early Times, Clarise's beverage of choice. The man had done his homework.

Billy trusted his instincts about the family. He knew the days of listening to his mother had largely passed for Jarvis. And the kid never had much of a relationship with his father, who drifted in and out from the start. Last time they spoke about it, Jarvis wasn't even sure where Charles was. The one thing they all knew was wherever Charles was, trouble was not far behind.

For the most part, Billy was the stabilizing force in Jarvis's life, and it had been that way for a while.

The agent flipped his phone down beside him on the couch and looked out across the water. Game day in Knoxville. The Vol Navy continued to strengthen and the anticipation built.

"You feeling it?" Billy said.

Rachel looked at him curiously. "Feeling what?"

"Never mind. Let's get ready to go over to the stadium, visit for a bit with some of our friends. I know they'll want to see you."

Now that he knew Clarise wouldn't be around, Billy could breathe a little easier. Too bad his team couldn't.

CHAPTER FOURTEEN

I t was getting late on the third Saturday in October, and the unexpected drama in Neyland Stadium was gripping the Vols and their legion of rabid fans.

Roll Damn Tide?

Not so fast.

Billy blended into the shimmering sea of orange, taking the occasional sip of Jack Daniel's from a tarnished flask with a Power T engraved on the side, a relic of his college days. He stared intently through binoculars as he sized up the considerable talent on the field.

Who might be persuaded to come his way?

As always, Jarvis was exceptional. He had already scored two early touchdowns – one that covered fifty-three yards and was ESPN highlight material, and another on a fade where he outmuscled the defensive back in the corner of the checkerboard end zone. He was headed toward double figures in catches.

The Autumn Blaze sure looked like a receiver poised for greatness at the next level. He was carrying his team.

The Vols were up 17-14 and driving again early in the fourth quarter when Jarvis broke free over the middle. Quarterback Stan Holsten hit him in stride and the play went the distance, forty-two yards. UT led by ten and the frenzy grew.

Alabama answered in typical fashion, hammering its way downfield for a short touchdown run by Fred Taylor. Again, the difference was a field goal. If its vaunted defense held, the mighty Crimson Tide could drive for the winning score at the end.

Most in the nervous crowd were certainly bracing for that. A decade of Alabama dominance had a way of shaping expectations.

But it didn't happen.

Facing a third-and-eight deep in his own territory, Holsten whipped a quick pass in the flat to Jarvis, who juked the first defender and broke toward the sideline. The Alabama safety had the angle, but Jarvis turned on the jets and easily shed the desperate grab at his shoulder pads at the first-down marker. One more quick cut and he was on his way. Eighty yards.

The Vols led again by two scores with just three minutes left, and the roar reverberated through all of college football. Number one was going down in Knoxville.

The huge throng, more than a hundred thousand strong, was deliriously happy. Thousands poured onto the field to celebrate as the clock expired, and Jarvis was quickly engulfed. As teammates paraded him around on their shoulders, the hero pointed up into the pulsating stands. Billy pointed back, for what it was worth.

For the day, Jarvis had twelve catches for two hundred thirty-six yards and four touchdowns, the best game of his career.

Billy took a long swig from his flask, turned to Rachel and shook his head in amazement. The noise was still deafening.

"Rocky Top!" he yelled.

She just smiled and pointed at her top. Voluptuous and, for the moment, a jubilant UT fan.

Reality would set in later for the home team. It was four-and-three on the season and would still have to fight to become bowl eligible. Coach Jack Stratton was still on the hot seat; his job likely hung in the balance of the last five games.

But tonight, with the epic upset in hand, Vol Nation would party hardy.

As an alleged fool who had again dared to take his alma mater and the points, Billy was prepared to buy drinks – lots of drinks – for his Alabama buddies down on the Strip that night. For once he'd be on the receiving end.

In the grand scheme of things, it was just another frenetic football weekend in SEC country, another chance for the agent to make connections and spread the gospel. The league was a fertile proving ground, and the most proven player of all belonged to him.

"Let's go back down to the river," Billy said as he shuffled to the exit with Rachel. "We'll grill that chicken and then hit the town for a little while. It's gonna be crazy."

"Are you sure your Tuscaloosa friends will show up?" Rachel said. "I'm guessing they're taking this kind of hard."

"Show up? Hell, they better show up and be men about it. We finally won, and I'm thirsty."

"What about Jarvis?"

"I'm sure he'll be the center of attention for the next few hours. This is his day, maybe the best day ever for a UT receiver. I don't know what his plans are, but we'll touch base with him before we head to the house."

Billy smiled and took another celebratory sip from the flask.

"Maybe we'll have some time to ourselves later," he said. "Right now, let's just enjoy this."

CHAPTER FIFTEEN

The End Zone was one of the popular joints along the six-block stretch of Cumberland Avenue known as the Strip, and it was filling up fast with rejoicing UT students. They were a resilient bunch that had learned over the last few years not to let losses get them down for long. No telling what kind of charge a signature win like this would put in them, but the bar's employees were bracing for a raucous night. The intensity showed on their faces.

Billy used to spend a lot of time here during his college days, between those bursts of academic focus, and he kept coming back. The food and drink were good, and the scenery was always interesting. Football was beaming in from everywhere on the big plasma TVs as he and Rachel sat down for drinks with a couple of the Alabama faithful. The visitors showed up, true to their word, but some others did not. Losing was too great a shock to their systems.

Billy got to know the two men sitting across from him when he was in law school and now saw them out on the SEC trail from time to time while he was scouting various players. He usually dreaded their visits to

Knoxville, especially when he was picking up the tab. Not tonight. This was his time to crow – and to drink for free.

"Well, I guess you're due to stumble into a win against us every decade or so," said the normally boisterous one in the crimson baseball cap.

"You have to admit, we looked pretty good out there today," Billy said. "There was no stumbling into anything."

"I *will* give you this: Jarvis Thompson is one hell of a player. If there's a better one out there in college football right now, I don't know who it is. With those hands and his size, he kind of reminds me of our man Julio Jones. And he's definitely faster. I'll be glad to see him playing on Sundays next year."

"So will I," Billy said. "So will I."

"Seems like a pretty classy kid, too. I like the way he handles himself. An agent's dream, right?"

"Great kid. Has a little family baggage, but I think we're about to work past that."

Rachel got up to use the restroom, and a lot of eyes followed her as she strutted across the spacious hall. Even in the dim light, she was an attention grabber.

"Gotta love those Charleston girls," the other Tide fan said, raising his glass in tribute.

Billy wasn't sure whether it was love or not, but he knew he wouldn't be where he was today without Rachel. Or her father, Bradley King.

King was a third-generation developer on Isle of Palms and a huge sports fan. He had invested generously in Billy's business at the beginning. The only condition,

besides the occasional game tickets and signed memora-
bilia and such, was that his daughter would be part of the
operation and well cared for.

Billy came from a fairly modest upbringing and
welcomed the financial backing. He had been given an
opportunity to take the ball and run. Now all he had
to do was make sure Rachel was content, which was no
simple chore.

But for the moment, things seemed to be going well.

"I could use another drink," Rachel said as she
returned to the table, bubbling with energy. "Are these
small glasses or what?"

Right on cue, a waitress approached with another
vodka tonic with a twist of lime and placed it in front of
Rachel. She looked at Billy.

"You already ordered me one? Thanks," she said. He
shook his head.

"From the gentleman in the booth over there," the
waitress said, nodding toward the darkest corner in the
joint.

They turned and strained to see, but the booth was
empty. A waitress was already starting to wipe down the
table for the next customer.

"He was there a minute ago," the waitress said.
"Long-haired guy with a beard. Said he thought you'd
need one."

"So some dude is hitting on you but can't stick
around long enough to see how things turn out," Billy
said. "Must have been an Alabama man. Not up to the
task today."

"I don't care who he was," Rachel said. "I'll take the drink."

The group enjoyed a couple more, and Billy's friends called it quits. They were looking at a long, depressing ride home. Losing to the Vols was simply unacceptable to any Alabama fan.

"See you guys down the road, definitely at Bryant-Denny next year," Billy said. "That'll be two in a row."

"Not without Jarvis it won't," said the one in the cap. "Better enjoy him while you can. Maybe he'll even get you into the Viagra Bowl or something, while we try to get back in the national championship hunt."

The receiver was probably waiting at the boat by now. Billy had spoken with him briefly, and Jarvis said he'd had enough celebrating with the masses.

He just wanted to get away for a while.

CHAPTER SIXTEEN

Eleven o'clock was approaching by the time Billy and Rachel reached the docks. On this starry night, euphoria continued to permeate the cool air. The Tide had been stemmed, finally, and the Vol Navy was going to savor every drunken moment. The massive football palace, beautifully lit, stood quiet in the distance as a half-moon hung overhead.

The path to Billy's houseboat was especially precarious under the circumstances.

"Damn Vols," said a crusty Navy regular sipping on a Budweiser as the couple passed his cruiser. "Been jerking us around all season ... who knew? That's the kind of team that can drive a man crazy. I didn't think I'd live long enough to see us beat 'Bama again. Jarvis was awesome."

"Enjoy it while you can, my friend," Billy said. "Missouri will be in here next week, and we'll probably be flatter than flat. We're still a long way from where we need to be."

"We're at least closer than we were when I started drinking this morning," the man said.

Billy laughed and jumped onto the deck of his boat. He extended a hand to Rachel, who stretched across and unlocked the cabin door. After a quick glance in the mirror, she flopped onto the couch and closed her eyes.

"Let me know when we arrive, captain," she said.

"What? Too much fun, party girl?"

Rachel's eyes opened quickly and a sultry expression came over her face. "You know better."

Billy wondered where she got all that energy, but he had no reason to complain. In fact, he had every reason to get home as soon as possible.

Leaving from the docks could be challenging late on a Saturday night, and it didn't take much of a mental lapse to cause problems with a big houseboat. They didn't need any problems tonight.

"Where's Jarvis?" Rachel asked.

Billy shrugged. "I thought he'd already be here. Probably got caught up in another crowd."

As he checked his watch, Billy noticed the tall figure in the distance, near the Big Orange Country sign. He was wearing a hoodie and baggy jeans and talking on a cell phone; it was definitely Jarvis, and he had his roommate with him.

Brett Sterling was a hard-hitting safety from California, a finely sculpted young man with a distinctive West Coast flair. His signature look was the long blond hair that he usually kept in a ponytail when it wasn't flowing freely from the back of his helmet. He could easily have passed for a model.

Despite vastly different backgrounds, he and Jarvis had been fast friends from the start at UT and were voted team co-captains before the season. They always set the right kind of examples.

Sterling was known to ride his bicycle everywhere – day or night, rain or shine, hot or cold – and was standing beside it now as he waited with Jarvis.

Billy held up a hand and called out. "Hey, ready to go?"

Jarvis squinted and stuck the phone in his pocket, and they began to walk Billy's way. Even in the shadows, their smiles were easy to see.

Billy reached out with an enthusiastic high five for each of the players as they approached the boat, and Jarvis climbed aboard. He tossed his black backpack with the orange number eleven stitching into the cabin.

"What a crazy day," he said. "So we gonna take a boat ride?"

"Getting ready to leave right now. Why don't you just stay over and I'll drive you back to your place in the morning. Did you ever hear from your mother?"

"I was just talking to her; she's still down in Florida. Said she didn't feel like traveling. No big surprise."

Billy didn't bother to respond, or mention the earlier phone call from Clarise. He figured it was best to let sleeping dogs lie, so to speak.

"How are you doing, Brett?" he said. "Want to go with us?"

"I better not. Already had a couple of beers up at Calhoun's and probably need to pedal on home. I've got things to take care of." He turned to his teammate. "Great game, Jarvis. Let's do it again next week."

"We're gonna make a run," Jarvis said. "Everybody around here better get ready. I'll see you tomorrow."

The receiver bounced into the cabin, and Rachel hopped up off the couch to give him a hug. "You played great," she said. "Want a beer?"

"Sure."

"Remember what I said about leaving a legacy?" Billy said. "You did that today. People around these parts will never forget you. You'll be able to come back and drink free beer for the rest of your life."

"Yeah, I got that impression tonight. Might even get a free meal or two."

"You know you can't be satisfied. This is a process, and there's still a lot of football to be played before you start doing commercials and shopping for sports cars. All in good time."

"Yessir, I hear you. Remember, I want a red one."

Billy cranked the engine, turned on the running lights and surveyed his exit route while Jarvis started freeing the boat from its Navy ties. The coast was clear. Billy eased it into gear and *Agent Orange* lumbered away into the darkness.

CHAPTER SEVENTEEN

It would be a smooth ride downriver, assuming they could avoid the water cops that kept a close eye on the area. Billy's brother, John, was supposed to be at the house waiting for them.

Billy took the wheel and pulled a celebratory cigar from the glove box. It had been waiting in there for a while. The sweet smoke wafted through the cabin as he drove.

"Jarvis, do you remember the first time we went out on this thing?" he said. "You didn't want to go."

"Hell, I'm scared of water, Billy. You know I can't swim. Still want a boat, though. Women like boats."

"Women like all kinds of expensive toys. Right, Rachel?"

She smiled.

"Seems odd for a strapping young man from the Gulf Coast to be afraid of the water," Billy said. "There's water everywhere down there."

"Yeah, but you don't want to be in a lot of it. There's some dangerous stuff in Florida water, alligators and snakes."

The houseboat purred along on the tranquil river, under the old railroad trestle with the blue lights and around the bend. It was a spectacular night, and there wouldn't be a more triumphant one this year in Vol Nation.

For the star player and his mentor, time was moving fast.

Jarvis would be a pro soon, on to bigger and better things in an NFL city somewhere. Billy would be making serious strides, too, maybe looking down on his man from some owner's luxury box. They would be a formidable combination for many years to come.

Still, Billy could never forget his father's words when he first broke the news that he was walking away from a lucrative legal career: "Counting on twenty-year-olds for much of anything is foolish. It sounds risky to me."

Coming from the Sevierville police chief, a man who had dodged a few bullets in his day, that had struck Billy as funny. But he knew it was true.

Courting college kids who had big dreams and the skills to match would always be dicey. Career decisions worth millions were often made on a whim – which way the wind, or cash, happened to be blowing on a given day. The agents were in charge, until they weren't.

Billy had learned to enjoy the intrigue of the chase, trying to close the deal, and his confidence had only grown in the last year with the prospects of Jarvis and some other SEC stars coming into the fold. In the sports business, one good signing often led to another. And a transcendent star could do wonders.

Once Jarvis was officially committed, the sky was the limit for Team Beckett.

"I hope we can do this some more," Billy said as the houseboat came into the home stretch. "It's been nice having you here the last couple of years."

"You know I'll be back," Jarvis said, "because I really like Rachel."

They all laughed.

Billy's house had a distinctive shine at night, with its tall, arching windows and stained-glass trim, the vaulted ceilings and the subtle lighting of the pool area reflecting off the stone walls. Amber landscaping lanterns ran down the steep hill to the water and accented the dock.

It was a million-dollar property in a neighborhood with much more expensive homes – one of the nicest belonged to the Vols' head coach – and Billy had to dig deep on the financing. He figured he'd grow into it.

The house was coming into view now, and Billy feathered back the throttle and pulled out his phone. "John, come down and catch us."

That drew a worrisome glance from Jarvis.

"John's here?" he said. "Does he know I'm with you?"

CHAPTER EIGHTEEN

John Beckett was not a happy man.

He had been part of the Billy Beckett Enterprises team from the start, and the whole routine was wearing thin. Nights like this didn't help.

"What took you so long?" he said as he got a hand on the railing and eased the big boat to its berth. "I've been sitting around here forever. Must have been a hellacious party."

"Oh, it's still going on," Billy said. "We could have stayed all night; definitely had plenty of company. I tried to get you to come with us."

"I just didn't feel like fooling with it."

"Well, too bad for you. The Vols pulled off the impossible, and our man here had a game for the ages. I'm predicting he'll be the national player of the week."

John barely gave the receiver a second look.

"With that kind of talent, seems like the team should be better," he said. "Must not be rubbing off."

"We've been scoring points," Jarvis said. "I can't play defense, too."

The exchange had a familiar edge. John and Jarvis had never been close, and the tension tended to flare easily.

"Have another beer and chill out, John," Rachel said as she headed up the walkway to the house. "This was a great day all around."

Chill out? That wasn't likely to happen. John's life had been in a tailspin for years and there was no relief in sight.

He was supposed to be pitching in some major-league ballpark, a big left-hander still in his prime. But he ran into arm trouble early in his junior year at Florida State, went through two surgeries and never made it back. John dropped out of school with no real backup plan, hardened by a new reality: the dream was over.

A bold FSU tattoo on his left bicep was a constant reminder a decade later. He often said, only half-kidding, it stood for Forgotten Screw-Up. Drug and alcohol problems had become more difficult to conceal, and the best John could do most days was run errands for Billy and try to stay out of trouble. Haunted by what might have been, he brooded constantly. Nothing could fill the void of being out there on the mound, in total command.

One thing was for sure: catering to these young studs on their way up was getting harder to do.

"Did you chart what all those SEC guys did today?" Billy said. "It was a big weekend and we need to stay on them. I'm probably going down to Florida next week for some meetings. I need you to handle a few things here, so be prepared."

John gritted his teeth. "I'll take care of it."

Big brother had thrown him a lifeline years ago, after John's career was ruined and everything was going to hell. He didn't have anywhere else to turn. He had moved in with his father, working odd jobs in Pigeon Forge and partying a little later every night. Cocaine was starting to creep into the mix.

If anybody could save him, it was Billy. He gave John a job and a new direction, a reason to stay clean, but the psychological damage had already been done in Tallahassee. Billy couldn't fix that.

"I saw where the 'Noles lost again today," Billy said. "There's some serious talent being wasted down there for sure. How many of those guys will be playing on Sundays next year? Six? Seven? I'm still hoping we'll end up with one or two of them."

"Tough times in Tallahassee," John said. "Imagine that."

There wasn't much that John wanted to remember about Florida State these days, and that included Jarvis Thompson. He had grown resentful of his brother's budding relationship with the receiver. And there was no turning back now.

"Jarvis, let's have a beer," he said, pulling a couple of deck chairs from a storage locker. "Better yet, a shot of tequila and then a beer. To hell with Alabama, we'll just throw a little NFL welcoming party right here under the stars. Let's see what the All-American is really made of."

John knew Jarvis wasn't much of a drinker and could tell the receiver had a good buzz going. That gave him the upper hand.

"Maybe for an hour or so," Jarvis said. "It's late and I gotta get back to work tomorrow, finish the season right. If we beat Missouri, we'll be close to making a bowl. That's important for Coach and the team."

"You boys still got Vandy and Kentucky left," John said. "That's always the beauty of November at UT; you've got two late wins built in there every year. You damn sure better make a bowl."

John looked over at Billy, who shook his head and walked toward the house.

"You guys carry on," he said. "I've got a date with Rachel that starts in about ten minutes. See you in the morning."

That brought a sly smile to John's face. Rachel had probably been through a gram of his coke by now, and she surely had plenty of energy to burn.

Another line or two and he wouldn't be feeling too bad himself.

CHAPTER NINETEEN

The phone was ringing off in the distance, and Billy gathered himself and rolled out of bed.

Lance Edwards, the UT receivers coach, was on the other end. He said Jarvis was supposed to meet him that morning for a sandwich and a film session in the Anderson Training Center, but he didn't show.

"Have you seen him?" Edwards asked.

"Not since last night. What's wrong?"

"He's not answering his phone, and his roommate said he didn't come home last night. Jarvis has never missed a meeting with me. How concerned should I be?"

"He probably stayed up late and wasn't moving too well this morning," Billy said. "Maybe he just forgot. I'll check around and see what I can find out."

Billy had always walked a fine line with the Vols' coaching staff. There was an understanding: he wouldn't get them into any trouble with the NCAA, and they wouldn't ask a lot of questions.

Jack Stratton, the head coach, was grateful that Jarvis was steered to Knoxville to begin with. He knew this would be their last season together and just wanted Billy to stay in the background until the appropriate time.

SCOTT PRATT

Like most coaches at major programs, Stratton understood agents were a necessary evil if you recruited players with designs on getting to the NFL. And if you weren't recruiting those players, you wouldn't be coaching long in the Southeastern Conference.

Billy wondered why Jarvis hadn't gotten him up earlier as he threw on a pair of jeans and a t-shirt. Rachel was still lying in bed, the sheets twisting around her body, and she pressed the pillow to her aching head.

"Wow. What's the problem?" she moaned. "They can't find Jarvis? He didn't mention anything about a meeting the last time I saw him."

"When was that?"

"Must have been about two o'clock. I went down to the dock and those guys were still going strong. You know Jarvis isn't used to hanging with John. It was cold and I didn't stay long. Hopefully he didn't pass out in the yard somewhere."

"Or fall in the river."

Billy looked through the house. The beds in all the guest rooms were still made. Maybe John gave Jarvis a ride somewhere late and didn't come home. They both should have known better than to be on the roads. Billy checked the driveway. John's old Range Rover was there.

Jarvis's cell phone again cut to voice mail, and Billy tried Brett Sterling. No answer. He called Edwards back and told the coach not to worry, that he'd track Jarvis down.

It was a sunny but cool day and a gentle breeze was blowing as Billy made his way down the path to the water. He was surprised to hear music pumping from the speakers on the boat, like the party was still in progress.

Through the cabin windows, Billy could see a few empty beer bottles scattered about and an open pint of tequila on the counter, with lemon slices and salt nearby.

"Hey, John!" he yelled.

Almost before the words were out of his mouth, he looked down and froze. There was his brother, sprawled out on the deck, eyes closed and blood trailing from the back of his head.

What the hell?

Billy rushed to John's side in a panic and quickly dialed Rachel's number. "Rachel!" he cried out. "Hurry down to the dock. John's in trouble."

Billy turned John's face toward him. It was bruised and swollen. The breaths were shallow and the pulse faint.

Come on, John! Come on!

Rachel scrambled down from the house a few minutes later, barefooted, wearing a pair of track shorts and an old t-shirt. She gasped.

"I already called 911," Billy said as he covered John with a blanket. "Ambulance is on the way."

He got up quickly to look for Jarvis in the back. The staterooms were empty.

Where could he be?

The paramedics took about fifteen minutes to arrive; it seemed like an hour. John was alive but in bad shape. Another fifteen minutes passed while the paramedics worked to stabilize him, got him ready for transport, hooked up oxygen and started an IV.

Billy was frantic by the time his brother was strapped to a board and carried up the hill to the waiting ambulance.

"Who did this?" he shouted to no one in particular. "Who would have had a reason? Where is Jarvis?"

PART II

CHAPTER TWENTY

The authorities descended on the river house with a flourish, and the mystery started to build.

A veteran Knoxville detective, Matthew Lewis, was on the case. He introduced himself to Billy and tried to shake the agent from his stupor.

"I'm sorry, Mr. Beckett," he said, "but we need to talk. Tell me what happened here."

"I don't know, detective." Billy's voice wavered. "I was asleep with my girlfriend at the house. My brother was down at the dock last night with a friend. That's the last I saw of him. We didn't hear a thing. I went down there late this morning and ... there he was, just lying on the boat like that."

"Who's the friend?"

"His name is Jarvis Thompson."

Billy could tell the detective knew that name; most people around Knoxville did. "The football player?" Lewis said. "Any idea where he went?"

"No, but I know he didn't do this. He and John were just down there drinking beer and listening to music, having a good time after the game. It was a huge day for Jarvis and the team. Nothing was wrong."

"Well, something obviously went bad wrong."

"I saw both of them at the dock about two o'clock," Rachel said. "There was a football game on the houseboat TV and they seemed to be getting along just fine."

"Were they drunk?" Lewis said.

"Maybe. Probably."

"What is your relationship to Jarvis Thompson?" the detective asked Billy. "Why was he here?"

"I've known him for years, since he was a kid down in Florida. I've kind of looked after him while he's been going to UT."

"What do you do for a living?"

"I'm a sports agent."

"So you're Jarvis Thompson's agent?"

"Not officially. Not yet."

Billy knew the questions had only begun, and that the news would travel fast. Social media would take the story and stretch it in every direction.

"I need to get to the hospital," he said. "First I have to call my father."

Franklin Beckett was used to flipping into crisis mode, but Billy knew the veteran cop wasn't prepared for another family crisis. Franklin's own health had been in recent decline, and he was still reeling in many ways from losing Anna. He had never remarried, was never even seen out on a serious date that anyone could remember. He was fully invested in his boys, trying to fill the void their mother left.

Anna had been the rock of the family, the one all her men could depend on. John was her special project. She soothed his high-strung personality, nurtured his special talents, kept him moving forward. John's troubles began to mount after the crash, slowly but surely. In recent years they had mushroomed.

Franklin's phone rang just as he was settling in to watch NFL games at home in Sevierville. Billy took a deep breath. He knew the news would floor his father. John may have been on shaky ground, but this was beyond their imagination.

"Your football star did this?" Franklin said, choking on the question. "Why?"

"I don't know, Dad. No one has seen Jarvis since last night. He had no reason."

"John always thought he was trouble. Why did you even leave them alone together like that? The fact he's missing says plenty, doesn't it?"

"I don't believe that," Billy said. "Jarvis has everything going for him. Why would he put himself in jeopardy for no reason?"

"We're talking about two guys who didn't like each other drinking by the river in the middle of the night. Anything could have happened. I see it all the time."

"Jarvis was happy," Billy said. "It was a celebration."

"Some celebration. Where the hell is he?"

"We'll find him. I'm sure he isn't far."

"I'll be at the hospital in less than an hour, son. I'll see you there."

Billy rubbed his eyes, looked out toward the river and tried to grasp what was happening. Detective Lewis was coming back up the walkway, and Billy and Rachel met him on the veranda.

The news was getting worse.

"Your brother had some drugs on him, a vial of cocaine, it looks like," Lewis said. "The paramedics said it's obvious he had been using last night. And it's not the kind of stuff we normally see around here. Very pure rocks apparently."

Billy took another deep breath. He was surprised, but only mildly.

"John used to have a problem," he said. "I thought it was behind him. I had no idea he was involved again."

He looked over at his girlfriend, who was staring blankly into the distance.

"Did you know that, Rachel? You've spent more time with John lately than I have."

"No. No idea."

"The UT backpack down on the boat, does that belong to Jarvis?" Lewis said. Billy nodded. "We found some cocaine in it, too. Looks like the same stuff. There was also three hundred dollars tucked into a pocket inside. Three crisp bills, just like the ones in the cabin drawer. Is something else going on here that I should know about?"

Billy shook his head. He was stunned.

"Not that I'm aware of," he said. "I don't deal in drugs, detective, and I didn't realize anybody else here did either."

"What about the money? There was another couple of hundreds in the drawer."

"I didn't have any money other than what was in my pocket. And I didn't give Jarvis anything."

"Well, someone did," Lewis said. "Or else he just found it somewhere. We're going to take a good look around your property. We've issued a BOLO for Jarvis Thompson; hopefully he'll turn up pretty quick. We'll be talking to his family and his coaches and whoever else there at the university. And I'll need you both to come downtown and give a statement."

"I'm an attorney," Billy said, "so I know the drill. I can tell you right now, though, that we're not guilty of anything here."

"Well, this doesn't look very good for any of you," Lewis said. "For all I know, you guys were sitting around snorting cocaine and drinking and got into a fight, for whatever reason. And now one of the best college football players in the country is missing."

Lewis raised an eyebrow. "You know how that's going to go over in Knoxville."

Rachel had a sick look on her face and said she needed to sit down.

"Do you have something else you want to tell me, ma'am?" the detective said.

"No, I'm just shocked by all this. It's unreal."

"We'll straighten it out," Billy said, "but I'm going to the hospital first. Once I know my brother is okay, we'll come straight to the station. You guys just need to find Jarvis."

CHAPTER TWENTY-ONE

John was in intensive care at Baptist Medical Center when Billy and Rachel arrived. He was stable and doctors expected him to survive.

The question was how soon he'd be able to explain how he ended up there.

The developing story was perfectly scripted for a public fascinated by sports heroes and scandal. *Star receiver missing after agent's brother found severely beaten at river property. Cocaine and cash discovered at scene.*

ESPN had already come out with a live SportsCenter report. Twitter, which was a fun past-time of Jarvis's, was exploding with speculation. His followers, more than two hundred thousand of them, were in a frenzy.

Is Jarvis running scared after leaving John Beckett to die?

Was he kidnapped?

Could he have ended up in the river and drowned?

Was he selling cocaine, or just using?

What did the UT coaches know?

What did Billy Beckett know?

The phone messages for Billy were coming in from all over. He noticed one from Stratton, the head coach, and several from his clients who were concerned.

There was another from Clarise Thompson, and he put the phone to his ear. "I knew you couldn't be trusted. Where's my son?"

Billy and Rachel took a seat in the waiting area and within minutes were approached by a man holding a notebook and recorder. Billy knew it was Trey Birchfield, a reporter for the *Knoxville Journal* who covered the police beat and had flushed out any number of misdeeds involving UT football players. He'd be all over this story.

Billy had spoken to him a time or two in the past, just casual talk about Jarvis and his future. Birchfield enjoyed sports and liked to talk. This time the conversation wouldn't be pleasant.

"Mr. Beckett, what was Jarvis Thompson doing at your house last night?" the reporter asked. "Do you know where he is?"

"I haven't seen Jarvis. Now, if you'll excuse me, I'm here to check on my brother."

Birchfield pressed on. "Does Jarvis spend a lot of time at your house?" he said.

"Trey, please. We'll talk later, I promise."

The media storm was gathering strength, and Billy needed to prepare for it. Once his father arrived, he and Rachel would go see the detective and try to sort out this mess. He at least needed to exonerate himself, if that were possible.

Rachel appeared to be in a funk through all the craziness that morning and had trouble even making eye contact with Billy.

"You gonna be okay?" he said.

"I don't know. This is a nightmare and I'm afraid things are only going to get worse. I don't want to be in the middle of it."

"Why would you be in the middle of it? You haven't done anything wrong."

"I just have a bad feeling. Maybe I need to go home to Charleston for a little while ... I don't know how to help John."

Rachel had what would be best described as an evolving relationship with Billy's brother. It was prickly in the beginning, full of jealousy and suspicion, each wanting to secure a bigger role in Billy's affairs. As business picked up, they found themselves spending more time together. The chill was beginning to break.

For the last year or so, Rachel had been more prominent in meet-and-greets, putting the company's best face forward for the families of prospective clients. John frequently accompanied her. He was engaging enough when he needed to be, and when it came to talking about the nuances of the games, no one had better insight.

The two had recently made a swing through the Florida hotbeds, from Miami to Gainesville to Tallahassee, and returned with renewed focus. Billy was pleased to see them working for the common good and learning to trust each other.

Now he was suddenly trying to keep his team from falling apart.

"I don't see any point in going to Charleston," Billy said. "There's no need to panic. The best thing you can do for John is to stick around here and help him pull through this. We all need you. We still have a business to run and a lot of other guys that are counting on us. We have to keep going."

John was listed in critical condition. He had suffered blunt-force trauma to the head and had a couple of deep gashes at the base of his skull. The doctors said he was lucky he didn't lose any more blood than he did.

Hopefully John would remember what happened when he came to. Everyone needed to know.

"What if those guys got into it and Jarvis ended up in the river?" Rachel said. "He couldn't swim out of that cold water. Hell, he couldn't swim at all."

"I told the cops this morning and they'll be looking along the banks in their boats, just in case," Billy said. "That's not something I care to think about right now."

They walked down the hall to a small coffee shop, ordered two cups and sat down.

"You look exhausted," Billy said. "Why don't you go home and get some rest. I'll wait here for Dad. He should be along any minute. I'll let you know when we hear something."

"What about the detective? He's expecting us."

"I'll call him. First things first."

"John's going to be all right, isn't he?"

"He's a tough guy," Billy said. "I'd just like to know what we're really dealing with here. Even if everybody is okay, the problems with the cocaine and cash aren't going away. The publicity from this could ruin me."

"You think somebody else is involved?" Rachel said.

"I have that feeling, but who would have known those guys were down there in the middle of the night? Jarvis doesn't come by the house that much and rarely stays over. His roommate was the only one who knew."

Rachel stood up and walked unsteadily toward the exit.

"Call me," she said. "I need to lay down."

CHAPTER TWENTY-TWO

There was a knock at the front door, and Brett Sterling was waiting on the other side. He had ridden out to Billy's house from campus to try to learn more about what happened to his best friend.

The concern on his face was palpable as Rachel motioned him into the den. She had been lying on the couch, and the dazed expression hadn't gone away.

"Is Billy here?" Sterling said.

"No, he's at the hospital. Come in."

"How's his brother?"

"They're not sure yet, but they think he's going to be okay," Rachel said. "He's lucky, I guess."

"Getting attacked in the middle of the night doesn't sound very lucky."

The two walked over to the couch and sat, and Sterling surveyed the surroundings. He had been in the house only once, maybe a year earlier. It was a late-night visit with Jarvis and another teammate. They crashed in the downstairs bedrooms and were up and gone early the next morning.

Sterling had always been leery about agents and the trouble that seemed to follow a lot of them. In his mind, they were best avoided.

"The police talked to me this morning," he said. "What happened here?"

"That's what we're all trying to figure out," Rachel said. "I take it you haven't heard from Jarvis."

"Not a word. We just had a team meeting, several of the older guys, and I can tell you a lot of people are freaking out over this. They're not happy with Billy for getting Jarvis involved."

"Billy didn't have anything to do with that and —."

"If Jarvis had just gone on home with me last night, we wouldn't be having this conversation. He always trusts Billy. Looks like it may have cost him this time."

Sterling shook his head and took a deep breath.

"This doesn't make any sense," he said. "I know him and Billy's brother aren't good friends, but Jarvis isn't a violent guy. And he's not into drugs either. I would know."

The players had lived together in an off-campus apartment for the past couple of years. It was a fairly quiet existence, classes and football mostly.

On the field they were stars, but both tried to keep a low profile away from the limelight, outside of social media. They had a small circle of friends and even distanced themselves from the pretty girls that were constantly coming around. Neither had a steady date. They didn't want any distractions, any trouble.

"Has Jarvis said anything lately about any problems, or anybody bothering him?" Rachel said.

"Nothing. He's been happier than ever. He knows the NFL is right down the road and has been playing his butt off. He's just been at peace with the whole situation. It's his dream."

"What about his family? Had he talked to any of them in the last few days?"

"Only his mother," Sterling said. "She calls fairly regularly and yanks his chain. That's about all she's good for."

"Do you know what they were talking about the last time?"

"Jarvis didn't say, but I could tell he was a little bothered by it. I got the impression it had something to do with that New Orleans agent she's been pushing. Jarvis had told me about that. I think he told Billy, too."

"So you think Clarise was pressing him about who he's going to sign with?"

"I'm sure it had something to do with money. She has some serious issues, and usually Jarvis just blows her off and goes on about his business. It's been that way as long as I've known him."

Sterling mentioned meeting Clarise last summer when he and Jarvis took a trip down to the Gulf. They were staying with another friend in Pensacola and dropped by the house in Autumn to pick up some old beach stuff that was stashed in a shed around back. Jarvis was in a hurry to get in and out. He made a quick introduction and they moved on.

Sterling was glad of that.

"How about something to drink?" Rachel said.

"Thanks. Anything cold would do. It's a pretty good ride out here."

Rachel returned from the kitchen with a couple of iced teas and sat back down on the couch.

"I know Jarvis loves you like a brother," she said. "He trusts you more than anybody on campus. Let me ask you, where do you think he is? What happened to him?"

"I don't know," Sterling said, "but I've got a bad feeling in my gut. He wasn't going to do anything to jeopardize his future. I mean, he's going to be a very rich man soon."

"Well, we need to find him. Today. Right now. Let us know if you hear anything at all."

Sterling quickly finished his tea, and Rachel walked him to the door.

"By the way, there wasn't much I could tell the police this morning," he said. "Except that I was with Jarvis after the game and he left with you guys on the boat. I told them we had a couple of beers and everything seemed fine."

"That's all right. Just the truth."

"They did ask me about the drugs, too," Sterling said. "They wondered if I had been using with Jarvis, or seen him using with someone else after the game. The cops also asked about Billy, how well I know him and how often I've seen him and Jarvis together. I didn't have anything bad to say, but he's not going to come out of this whole thing looking good."

"Let's just hope Jarvis is okay. We'll deal with the rest of it as it comes."

Rachel stood on the porch and watched as Sterling mounted his bike and pedaled away. Within moments, she was dialing on her phone.

"Call me as soon as you get this," she said. "We need to talk."

CHAPTER TWENTY-THREE

The patient slowly lifted his gaze and took in the muted surroundings of Tranquility Bay.

After a week at the drug rehab center near Panama City, Florida, his mind was beginning to clear.

Detoxification, the first step in a twenty-eight-day, in-patient treatment program was behind him now. Still to come, according to the poster on the wall: therapeutic intervention, life skills development, and relapse prevention.

Life skills development? Dante Thompson chuckled to himself. What appreciable skills might a black man from the projects develop after years of trafficking cocaine?

"How do you feel today, Dante?"

The bespectacled counselor with gray hair and a neatly trimmed beard smiled as he waited for the answer. He was sitting behind a desk that took up much of his small office, directly across from his haggard patient.

"Okay," Dante said. "Better."

The man flipped through the patient's file with a nod. He said his name was Donald Cameron, and that he would be monitoring Dante's progress at the state facility. For better or worse.

Cameron scanned the paperwork like he'd apparently done for countless wayward souls through the years. Another addict who was battling tall odds was temporarily in his care.

"I just want you to know that we care about you here," Cameron said. "We want you to get better."

The spiel sounded to Dante like a reflex action by the counselor. Outside of coaches, he hadn't experienced much caring in his life. He had, in fact, been pretty much on his own from the beginning.

Before he was ten, he was drinking and smoking pot with his mother. The descent had begun. His skills as an athlete set him apart, helped him escape several scrapes with the law as a teen-ager. But he was clearly traveling a dangerous path.

Not even a baseball scholarship to Florida State was enough to turn him around. Dante was eventually kicked off the team for failing too many drug tests. He dropped out of school and out of sight, leaving his two younger siblings to fend for themselves. *If he couldn't see to himself, how could he help them?* The guilt just added to his burden.

For the last several years, Dante had reverted back to selling cocaine – his father's legacy – as part of a gang that operated in the Panama City area. Fortunately, he had avoided being killed along the way, or serving a long jail sentence. Instead, he became just one more addict on the streets.

Now, finally, Dante was being forced to dry out and start coming to grips with his stark reality.

"We haven't really had a chance to talk," the counselor was saying. "When they brought you in here, you were in pretty bad shape. Where were you going?"

"I was looking for my father."

"Where is he?"

Dante stared at the clock on the wall and tried harder to focus. *What day was it?* He spoke haltingly.

"I don't know. He's been missing for a while. I heard he was in New Orleans, but I couldn't find him. Then I heard he was dead. I just wanted to be sure."

"How did you end up here? I mean, I know how you ended up *here.* A lot of people the police come across in your condition end up here. But why were you in Panama City?"

"My father used to have friends here."

"Do you have any other family members?" Cameron said. "I understand you're from a small town up the road. You seem to be getting around."

"I haven't lived in Autumn in a while. My mother is still there. I have a younger brother who moved away and a sister ..."

"Where is she?"

"I don't know. We never found her."

"So she's missing, too? It's usually helpful when patients have a supportive family, someone they can count on. We'd like to let them know."

Supportive family? Dante couldn't grasp the concept.

"My mother is in worse shape than I am," he said. "I talk to my brother every now and then. He's a college football player."

"Where does he play?"

"Tennessee. Jarvis Thompson, All-American receiver. He's the only real man in the family."

"Why do you say that?"

"He's the only one who was strong enough to get away and stay away."

"Maybe we can get in touch with Jarvis, let him know what's going on with you. I'm sure he'd want to help."

"I don't want him to know. He'd be disappointed. I was supposed to be better than this. I had my chance and wasted it."

Cameron closed the case folder and dropped it on his desk. He smiled that detached smile, again.

"This is a process, Dante, and it's not easy, as you've probably already discovered," he said. "But we're going to help you work through it and get on with your life, maybe find a job. Getting well takes time, and you have to want it. You have to be strong."

"Right. Strong."

"We try to work together here. We have a group therapy session this morning, down the hall in our main conference room, and I'd like for you to join us. Starts in fifteen minutes. We just get to know each other a little better."

"I'm not looking to make new friends."

"It's about support. Trust me, it'll be good for you. If you want, you can wait out in the main hall and watch TV until we're ready. It usually stays on one of the sports channels this time of year, because most everybody around here but me is into football. You like sports?"

"I used to."

"I'll let you know when it's time."

Dante got up and shuffled out the door, toward the television in the far corner of the big room. He couldn't believe his blurry eyes as he got closer. A headshot of his brother was on the screen behind the SportsCenter host, who was talking away. *Missing Receiver*, the caption said.

Missing?

Dante quickly found the remote control and turned up the volume. He was able to catch the last of it.

Knoxville police are currently looking for Thompson, who caught four touchdown passes in the Vols' upset of top-ranked Alabama on Saturday. The agent's brother remains in critical condition in a Knoxville hospital.

The blood started to rush to his head, and Dante dropped into the nearest chair to digest the news. So Jarvis had snapped and was on the run? It didn't seem possible.

Ten minutes until group therapy.

Dante got up again and began walking down the residence hall. By the time he reached his room, he was almost running.

CHAPTER TWENTY-FOUR

Billy's demeanor in the heat of battle had always impressed colleagues. He was measured, analytical, on point.

He could take a complex legal case and break it down, make it seem simple and be thoroughly convincing. Or he could start with the most basic premise and inflate it into something grand to fit his point of view. A master salesman, they called him.

That approach had carried him near the top of his class in law school and earned him a reputation as a young attorney to watch in Atlanta. If anyone seemed destined to blossom into a courtroom star, it was Billy. The evidence was mounting.

A few years into his career, his law firm had become involved in a lengthy, well-publicized fraud investigation known as the Allied Global Shipping case. Several companies doing business in the Gulf of Mexico had been losing millions of dollars, and officials couldn't figure out why. The case soon became a cocktail of crooked politicians, accountants, lawyers, and various state and federal agencies.

Billy, with his keen attention to detail, had been brought in from Atlanta to assist a legal team, and within a few days deduced how a crime ring had been using duplicate cargo lists and a few well-placed employees to cook the books. In hindsight, it was a simple scheme, but no one else had seen it. The operation, which had been going on for years, was shut down and its leaders sent to prison.

Billy was hailed for his role and offered a lucrative promotion at his firm. His professional future was set. But instead of cashing in, within months he defied conventional wisdom again and went back to his first love. Sports.

It seemed like a perfectly foolish choice now as he slumped at his desk to assess the damage of the impending Jarvis Thompson fiasco.

One of the best college football players in the nation had simply disappeared. His brother was nearly beaten to death. There was the cocaine and the cash. And all of it at Billy's own house, right under his nose.

If the public wasn't already suspicious enough of sports agents and their games, this should set everybody in the profession back a few notches.

Billy was keenly aware that image was everything when it came to representing high-profile athletes. Yes, perceptions mattered. He had thrived with that basic premise. Now he had to wonder whether his business could survive the brewing scandal.

Sitting in his office, with messages streaming in and the media spotlight getting hotter by the hour, Billy needed to come up with his best plan yet. It started with Mark Fletcher, the private investigator in Atlanta. If anyone could help bring some perspective and order to the situation, it was Fletcher.

"Sorry to bother you again, man, but I've got big troubles here," Billy said.

"I heard," Fletcher said. "I was getting ready to call. How can I help?"

"I have to pick up a trail on Jarvis. I just hope there's one out there. This is more bizarre than anything I've ever run across."

"What's your read on the situation? Did Jarvis do this to your brother?"

"I don't believe it, but the circumstances aren't good, and his background makes him look capable. Or somebody could have showed up in the middle of the night, out of nowhere, and beaten up John and taken Jarvis. Seems pretty farfetched; those are two big boys you wouldn't want to mess with. But who knows what to think at this point? Jarvis could be dead for all I know. Could have drowned even."

"Let's think positive here," Fletcher said. "If he didn't do it and isn't dead, he can't be too far away. But that means other people are involved. Bad people, obviously."

"What I'm wondering," Billy said, "is whether the things we talked about last time may be coming into play somehow."

"What do you mean?"

"I mean somebody is sending a message here, a very pointed message. Jarvis is a victim, just like my brother. He's out there, somewhere."

"You talking about Sonny Bradley?" Fletcher said. "I can't imagine even a sleaze like him playing this kind of game. This is dead serious. The whole country is watching."

"If not him, the guy who is calling the shots down there. Frank Romano. I'll bet he's not above this kind of in-your-face caper."

There was a pause and Fletcher sounded intrigued.

"So what can I do that the police can't?" he said.

"I think this all starts down in Florida and extends back to New Orleans. There are a lot of people with an interest in Jarvis, in his future earning power. His mother would be right at the top of the list. While the cops are checking everything up here, why don't you see what you can find out about his family. Clarise, Dante, Charles … any of them could be involved in this somehow. Maybe all of them are."

"I have to be here day after tomorrow to take care of some personal business, but I can be down in Florida in just a few hours and start digging. Might find out something quick. I'll throw some stuff in a bag and take off now."

"I would appreciate it, Mark. My career may be riding on how this plays out."

"When will I hear from you again?"

"I'm waiting to see how my brother comes out of this first. If he's going to be all right and we still haven't heard anything from Jarvis, I probably need to pay Clarise a visit. I'm sure she'll be thrilled to see me. I'll call you late tomorrow."

"Let's hope the situation clears up before you have to do that," Fletcher said. "Just let me know."

CHAPTER TWENTY-FIVE

The front-page headline in *USA Today* said it all: *Where is Jarvis Thompson?*

Billy tossed the newspaper aside and stared out the window on a morning flight to Pensacola. From there he'd rent a car and make the short drive over to Autumn. Clarise Thompson would be waiting.

Billy had never dreaded a trip more than this one. Clarise's mood swings were unpredictable under the best of circumstances. Add this kind of stress, where her fantasies were hanging in the balance, and anything was possible.

He just needed to look into her glassy eyes, see if she knew anything, try to figure out what she was up to.

Even now, with Jarvis missing and everything in limbo, Clarise was working on her own twisted agenda. Billy was sure of that.

The winds off the Gulf were picking up, and it looked like a storm was moving in as the small prop plane made its choppy descent into Pensacola. The last time Billy flew down, when he visited Autumn three years ago, it was quite the memorable occasion. Jarvis had decided to go to Tennessee and play football, an announcement that resonated across the country. But there was no celebration in the Thompson household. Clarise hated the idea. She wanted her son at Florida State, still in her little sphere of influence.

When Billy showed up at the door with an armful of orange UT garb, you would have thought the devil himself was making a house call.

He had already intervened more than once to try to keep the pride of Autumn on the right track. Considering all the forces that conspired against him, it was amazing Jarvis was still in his camp. The family had always been like a train wreck playing out in slow motion, with plenty of casualties.

The agent pulled his lap belt tight. He knew full well the characters he was dealing with.

Clarise surely fit the clinical definition of a sociopath. She was never capable of loving anyone other than herself, even before the bleakness and desperation had taken hold of her life. Now it was far too late.

Dante, the eldest son, was smart and a talented athlete. He had a chance to make something of himself but ended up a broken man, a drug dealer who flamed out in his attempt to earn a legitimate living.

For his part, father Charles periodically showed up at the house with a variety of substance abuse problems on full display. A quiet and fatalistic man, he'd usually crash for the night and move on. There was little emotional attachment.

It was always that way with Charles. His relationship with Clarise produced three children but was nothing more than an intermittent series of one-night stands, fueled by alcohol and drugs. They were divorced before Dante was even born, and she made sure none of their children would ever be saddled with the Ratliff name.

Apparently, Clarise hadn't noticed the growing stigma of being a Thompson in Autumn, Florida.

Somehow Jarvis managed to avoid most of the lethal pitfalls. But trouble, serious trouble, was always lurking in the neighborhood.

Billy barely noticed the plane touching down as he flashed back to the night the whole thing hit bottom, when Denise Rollins was killed in front of the house. Jarvis had been on his phone and let her leave without an escort. A passing car screeched to a halt near Denise. A man leaned out the back passenger window and fired three shots.

Jarvis was ready to take up arms himself when he made the panic-stricken call just before midnight, but Billy talked him out of it and got in his car and drove all night from Tennessee. By then it was painfully clear that football was Jarvis's only chance to get away, and if things weren't handled right, football wouldn't be enough to save him.

"You're better than this," Billy told him at Denise's funeral. "You've got so many things going for you … don't let these people ruin your life. I can help you, and I'll always be there."

A year later, Jarvis was in Knoxville.

CHAPTER TWENTY-SIX

Billy made his way along the East Bay loop, past the old plantation estates that showed the best side of Autumn and on through the quaint downtown area. He was headed to the other side of the tracks at the far end of town.

The dilapidated gray house on Bright Street, a misnomer if there ever was one, was in even worse shape than he imagined. The roof was missing shingles, the siding was splintered. What little paint that remained on the trim was in the process of flaking off. A few of the shutters had long since fallen and were obscured by knee-high weeds.

The inside of the house surely had to be a living hell, Billy thought. He wondered how Jarvis, or anybody else, could call this place home.

The skies were starting to spit rain as he walked up the broken sidewalk, past the spot where Denise had been killed. Hopefully, he thought, this wouldn't be one of those torrential Florida downpours. Billy opened the aluminum storm door, which had no glass and was at the mercy of the shifting wind, and knocked loudly.

After a couple of minutes, Clarise appeared. She looked surprised to have a visitor in the middle of the day. And this was certainly not one she wanted to entertain.

She was a large woman wearing a faded blue bathrobe over a nightgown that she could have had on for days. The hateful expression on her face was even more pronounced with Billy suddenly at her door, and it didn't take her long to start in.

"Where the hell is my son?" she snapped. "I thought you were supposed to be looking after him. And now he disappears from your own house and there's drugs all around. And you're giving him money, too. You never gave *me* any. You're one hell of an agent."

Clarise glared, long and hard. Billy could tell she had already been drinking that morning, but he expected that. He calmly stood his ground.

"Good to see you, too, Clarise," he said. "Mind if I come in?"

"Yes I do mind. There's nothing for you to do here. You've made a big enough mess already."

"I'm just trying to find Jarvis. You don't have any idea where he might be? I thought maybe something had gotten back to you from your friends down here."

"He don't call me much anymore," Clarise said. "You know that."

"But you call *him*. I know a few days ago you were still trying to talk him into signing with Sonny Bradley."

"So?"

"What's that guy going to do for you? I can tell you, those New Orleans gangsters are bad news. They don't care about Jarvis, and they sure don't care about you."

"They'll do more than you ever will," she said.

"Is it possible they're involved with his disappearance?"

"I'd say it's more possible that you are involved. I haven't trusted you since you took out that insurance policy."

Here we go again, Billy thought.

"That was for his own protection, Clarise," he said. "We've been over that a few times. I was his guardian, because of your state of mind, which doesn't seem to be getting any better, and we wanted to insure him against any disabling injuries. It has nothing to do with this."

"What's going to happen to me if he don't turn up and play football again? Jarvis was supposed to take care of me. He said he would."

This was the way conversations went with Clarise. Always the victim. It didn't take long for Billy to get his fill this time. He had to fight the urge to grab her by the throat.

"You're a selfish woman," he said. "I'm looking out for Jarvis, like I always have. For some reason, that isn't good enough for you."

"You're just a con man, Billy. Jarvis is going to make you a lot of money, and you know it. That's the only reason you're here now."

Billy took a deep breath and tried to collect himself. He hadn't come all the way down here to stand in the rain and trade insults with a drunk.

"Clarise, let's just get to the bottom line here," he said. "Your son is missing and we don't know what happened to him. Do you know of anyone who wanted to hurt him?"

"Hurt him? Everybody loves Jarvis. It's always been that way. He's a good boy ... even that lowlife father of his cares about him. And he don't care about much of anything."

"Where is Charles, anyway?" Billy asked. "This whole thing feels like something he might be involved in. Or is he back in prison again?"

"I have no idea, but I heard he was in New Orleans a while back. I don't want him around here. He's never been nothing but trouble."

"What about Dante?"

"Haven't seen him in weeks."

"There's just trouble everywhere you turn here," Billy said. "You should be grateful that Jarvis escaped this hellhole."

Clarise staggered and tried to slam the door, but Billy shoved it back in her face.

"For what it's worth, this isn't just about Jarvis," he said. "I've got a brother who's lying up in the hospital in Tennessee. I'm trying hard to believe that it wasn't Jarvis who put him there."

"You know better than that, Billy. You just find my son and get him back on the field. I got nothing else to say to you."

The door closed and Billy walked back to the car. He knew he hadn't seen the last of Clarise, unless she just dropped over dead. That was too much to hope for.

Billy rubbed his hands through his wet hair and picked up his phone. Mark Fletcher had left a message.

The private eye was checking around and sounded like he might have turned up something. He was anxious to talk about the case.

Billy decided to spend the night in Pensacola and see where the leads might take them.

CHAPTER TWENTY-SEVEN

Before he left Autumn, Billy wanted to talk to Ed Shelton, Jarvis's high school coach. They hadn't spoken in person since the tragic night that Denise Rollins was killed, but he knew Shelton would be keeping up with the Thompsons and all their drama. He used to take Jarvis in when times got really tough and Clarise was near her breaking point. If anyone in Autumn was looking out for the kid's best interests, it was his old coach.

Billy glanced at his watch. The high school was only a couple of blocks over, and he figured Shelton was probably getting ready for practice.

The rain had stopped and the players were on the field stretching when Billy walked up from the parking lot. Shelton noticed him immediately and cut him off at the sidelines with a stern look.

"Hello, Billy," he said. "Sorry to hear about Jarvis, and your brother, too. I take it there's nothing new today?"

"Nothing yet."

"Why are you here?"

"I don't want to interfere with your practice, coach, but I was hoping we could go down here and talk for a few minutes before you get started. I'll make it quick."

Shelton instructed an assistant to take over, and the men walked to the far end of the field and into the bleachers behind the end zone. They didn't bother to sit.

"Please tell me how you could allow this to happen," Shelton said, becoming more animated. "Jarvis had to go through so much to get where he is. He's a hero to these young players; I use him as an example all the time of how their lives can be better if they stay out of trouble and work hard. How does he end up in a situation like this?"

"We're all looking for answers right now. We don't even know exactly what the situation is. I just left his mother's house, and she acted completely clueless. I think she knows more than she's letting on, although it's always hard to tell."

"You know dealing with Clarise is a waste of time."

"I had to make the effort under the circumstances," Billy said. "You have your finger on the pulse here, Ed. You know what people are doing and thinking. What can you tell me?"

"Not much. I certainly have no idea where Jarvis is, or what happened to him. I do know that some guy from New Orleans was down here recently. Supposedly an agent that visited with Clarise. I also heard that Charles had been back in the area not too long ago. That's another bad sign."

Billy stared out at Shelton's players as they lined up for drills.

The Eagles were a perennial power in the region and typically had a handful of players sign major-college scholarships each year. Few were as coveted as Jarvis, who had led the team to state prominence, but Shelton treated them all the same.

Billy could tell they were wary of the stranger who was distracting their coach, interrupting his strict practice schedule.

"I won't take any more of your time," Billy said. "Please let me know if anything comes up. Anything at all."

Shelton managed a half-hearted smile, pulled the whistle from his pocket and started to walk toward the field. Back to work.

He stopped for a final thought.

"I don't know if I'd stick around town for long if I were you," he said.

That caught Billy by surprise. "What do you mean?"

"I mean, this town has been heavily invested in Jarvis for a long time. He's special. Some of the people didn't like to see him going off to Tennessee to play ball to begin with. Most have accepted it by now; they can see he's headed for big things, and they'll be proud when he's representing Autumn in the NFL. They'll feel like they're part of it. But now, all of a sudden, Jarvis is missing and who knows what's going to happen."

"So it's my fault?" Billy said.

"I'm not saying that. Just thought you might not want to linger too long down here. We're a small community, but we have our share of crazies."

"For what it's worth, Ed, I'm not a very popular guy in Tennessee right now either."

"I can appreciate that. I'm sorry you're in this mess. Really."

"You have to know I'll do anything to find Jarvis and get him back on track. Forget football, he's like a little brother to me."

Shelton looked Billy straight in the eye.

"I hope that's enough," he said. "I have to be honest with you, man, I thought going to Knoxville would be the best thing that ever happened to that kid. It got him out of that cesspool he grew up in, away from his mother. But now I don't know. This is bad."

CHAPTER TWENTY-EIGHT

Sonny Bradley stirred up a cloud of dust as he wheeled into the parking lot of an old warehouse down on the New Orleans waterfront.

Red-faced, he sprang from the car in a huff and strode quickly toward a side entrance. He didn't get far. Three men intercepted Bradley at the door and escorted him into the building. He was in no mood for interference.

"What's going on, Frank?" he barked as he burst into the office.

One of the men put a hand on Bradley's shoulder and stopped him in his tracks. Frank Romano just smiled as he leaned back in his big chair at the far end of the smoky room.

"It's all right," he said with a nod. "Let Sonny have his say."

The agent caught his breath and took a seat across the table from Romano, who casually lit another cigarette.

"This thing with Jarvis Thompson has gotten way out of hand," Bradley said. "I've had reporters calling me and asking me all sorts of questions. The NFL people are suddenly a lot more interested in what we're doing down here. There's plenty of trouble brewing. It's just not worth it."

"Not worth it?" Romano said. "We've been backing this little sports business of yours, building it up, and now it's not worth it?"

"Not if it all comes crashing down on my head," Bradley said. "I thought we were just trying to steal the kid away from Billy Beckett, you know, give ourselves a big-time client in the NFL for years to come. Now he's missing, Beckett's brother is damn near dead, and the whole country is wondering what happened. It's only a matter of time before this all comes home to roost. That's just common sense."

Romano leaned forward and glared at Bradley with a clenched jaw. There was fire in his eyes.

"I run the show here," he roared, pounding the table with his fist. "I'll decide how this plays out. We're going to be a player in everything around here, with or without you. If you can't sit tight, maybe I'm backing the wrong guy. You know I've got other options. Always."

The agent suddenly turned meek. Crossing Frank Romano was never a smart play.

"I just don't understand why all the bother over this one kid," he said. "It's college football, for God's sake. There are a lot of other great players out there. Why can't we just make our money and go about business quietly? We know a lot of people, and we've been doing good."

"Good ain't good enough," Romano said. "Jarvis Thompson is different; he's a superstar, and I have a special interest in him. That's not going to change."

"Then what happened to him?"

Romano sat back. "You don't want to know," he said. "You just go back to town and let me handle things.

Stay calm and keep your mouth shut. You don't know anything."

"Maybe not, but a lot of people are looking for him. I heard this morning that his brother has already been contacting some of our acquaintances in Florida, checking around."

"How do you know that?"

"They called me and told me about it. It's the same ones who said he'd been trying to find his old man earlier. I believe his name is Dante. Supposedly crashed and was in rehab somewhere in Florida. Looks like he's out and running loose again."

"If he's like his old man, he's a doper that can be easily dealt with. I've got more important things to worry about."

"No doubt about that. This is turning into an international incident. Why would you bring that on yourself? On all of us?"

"That's enough. You're getting paranoid, and that's never a healthy thing. I told you to just let me worry about it. It'll all work out fine in the end."

"If you say so, Frank. There are just a lot of loose ends. I hope you can tie them all up and we can move on. I'm not going to be the fall guy here."

Bradley got up and left the room, and Romano started to smile. That made his men smile, too.

"You guys go outside," he said. "Sonny seemed awfully nervous. Make sure he gets home safely."

CHAPTER TWENTY-NINE

The yellow Hummer stood out like a beacon as it circled the block and pulled to the curb in front of a ramshackle collection of row houses.

The two men on the corner looked around warily, checking for cops or other signs of trouble before approaching the driver's window. Rich people cruised through the neighborhood all the time, looking to score drugs, and this had all the markings of a quick transaction.

The heavily tinted glass slid down, and a smile broke out on the smaller man's face.

"Look at you," he said. "Where in the hell did you get *this*?"

Dante Thompson took a draw of his cigarette and grinned. "Just taking it for a test drive. Get in."

"Shotgun," said the man, who hurried around to the other side of the vehicle while his friend slid into the back seat. Dante flipped his cigarette butt into the street and sped away.

"Brother, I thought you were drying out somewhere," said the man in the back. "Didn't think we'd see you back in Pensacola for a while."

"I didn't either. Something came up and I need to talk to you boys. If I can count on anybody, it's T.J. and Isaac. Right?"

T.J., the passenger in front, pursed his lips. "Let me guess. This has to do with your brother. He's all over the news. They say he went off on some guy up in Tennessee, after the game. Or else somebody snatched him and made it look that way. Which is it?"

"Jarvis isn't stupid; he's going to the NFL," Dante said. "He's not like some other fools down here. I've been talking to his roommate, and he's sure Jarvis was kidnapped from his agent's house there on the river. He thinks the whole thing was set up."

"Set up by *who?*"

"I have an idea, but we need to be sure."

"*We?*" T.J. said. "What are you trying to pull, Dante?"

"Getting ready to take a little trip and set things right. If the cops can't do it, can't find him, I will. But I need some extra muscle. You boys owe me."

"Are you talking about those guys in New Orleans that killed your father? I don't know, man. We have gangs here, but that's a different deal. That's mafia."

"And that's why it might take a little more firepower than usual. Isaac, look behind you, under the tarp."

Isaac leaned over the seat and pulled back the black cover. He shook his head.

"What is it?" T.J. said.

"Looks like about five or six AKs. And if I'm not mistaken, there's some grenades in a box."

"*Grenades?* That's a lot more firepower than anything we've ever gotten involved in. What have you dreamed up this time?"

"Simple. Jarvis is out there somewhere and we have to track him down. For some added motivation, I've got something else that might be helpful. Look in the glove box, T.J."

The door opened and there was a gleaming baggie of white powder, almost two fingers deep. "I know how much you boys love the blow."

The passengers looked at each other with growing interest. They knew from experience that following Dante anywhere was risky. But he always managed to escape unscathed, charmed in some odd way. Besides, riding around in a nice car and getting high was better than standing on a street corner in Pensacola, waiting to get shot or arrested.

"So we're going to go cruising around looking for gangsters in a bright yellow Hummer, with a big sack of dust and a bunch of AKs and grenades?" T.J. said. "What could possibly go wrong?"

Dante smiled. "I'll get another car, so we don't stand out so much. Just three brothers minding their own business."

"I thought you were off the blow, Dante? Sounds like you're crazier than ever."

"I'm clean as a whistle right now, and it feels pretty good. My counselor would be proud. On the other hand, he's probably pissed about his Hummer."

Dante circled around the block again and let the men out where he picked them up.

"I'll be back in two hours," he said. "Be ready."

CHAPTER THIRTY

Reporters were starting to circulate around Autumn and ask a lot of questions. Mark Fletcher was already ahead of the game. The private investigator had spent the day talking to acquaintances of the Thompson family, in particular to friends of Dante. Once cocaine became part of the story, Jarvis's older brother was suddenly a person of interest.

Fletcher was on his way back to Atlanta when he called Billy, who had stopped out on the edge of Pensacola.

"Nobody sees much of Dante these days," Fletcher said, "but he's apparently still doing his thing. I hear his old man got him involved in the cocaine business back in high school, and he never got it out of his system."

Like Charles, Dante would come and go from the family home. Unlike the old man, he tried to look after Jarvis as much as possible. The brothers were still close until Jarvis left for college.

"I always got along well with Dante – he was good to Jarvis, helped keep him out of trouble – but it was hard to get close to him," Billy said. "He ran with a rough crowd, and you just never knew exactly what he was thinking."

"What are the chances he might be involved in this?"

"I'm sure he wouldn't intentionally sabotage his brother's future, but the cocaine begs the question. Where did it come from?"

"Didn't they have a sister?"

"She disappeared years ago in Texas. Presumed dead."

Billy looked up to find a wide-eyed waitress standing at his table with pad in hand. He ordered a cheeseburger, no onions, fries and the local brew of the day.

"What about Charles?" he said. "When was the last time anybody saw that worthless bastard?"

"He hasn't been around here in a couple of weeks at least. He supposedly was hanging out in New Orleans, but who knows? One guy said he didn't think Jarvis even talks to him anymore."

Billy was getting another call and put Fletcher on hold. It was Rachel. She was still at the hospital with his father.

"How's John?" he said.

"They think he may be coming around, but he's not talking yet."

"What about Dad?"

"He's right here. Has been the whole time," she said. "He's not taking this well. And it's not just John; he's worried about you, too."

"Tell him I'm trying to figure all this out and will be back as soon as I can. Probably tomorrow."

Rachel was feeling numb, she said, and then a long pause.

"We've been getting some calls at the office, too. Several of your guys are concerned about this publicity and said they couldn't get hold of you. It doesn't look good, and things are only going to get worse for business if Jarvis doesn't show up soon and have a great explanation."

"I know. I've got a bunch of messages on my phone. Just tell them not to worry, that I'm taking care of things. Tell them I'll be in touch soon."

"I'm not sure that's going to be enough," Rachel said.

"For right now, it'll have to be."

Billy flipped back over to Fletcher and shook his head as the waitress set a napkin and cold draft on his table.

"How did I get into this, Mark?" he said. "I'm so turned around, I don't even know what direction I'm going. And the floodwaters are rising. Any suggestions?"

"Well, if somebody else was involved in this thing at your house, I'm guessing they're tied to the Gulf – Florida or New Orleans, like you said," Fletcher said. "It just seems like a lot of things lead that way."

Another call beeped in, and Billy took a quick glance at the ID. He didn't recognize the number and let it go to voice mail with all the others.

"I'm heading back to Tennessee in the morning," he said, "but I want you to stay on this as long as it takes. If you need to chase it to New Orleans, do it. Hopefully we'll get a break."

"It's a different world over there," Fletcher said, "but I know the landscape pretty well. I think I can get a quick read on the situation, once I get down there. This business in Atlanta shouldn't take long."

"Just be careful. We've got some bad actors in this play."

"The world is full of them. I'll talk to you soon."

Billy had plenty to ponder as he finished his meal and threw a twenty on the table. He planned to get a motel room just up the road near the airport and catch an early flight home.

As he walked out of the restaurant, he noticed a couple of young men sitting in a white sedan, parked a few rows away. They were paying close attention to him, it seemed. *Am I getting paranoid now?* he wondered.

Billy slid into his rental car and tapped on the last message: "*Hello, Mr. Beckett, this is Trey Birchfield. Would you give me a call? I think I have something that will interest you.*"

CHAPTER THIRTY-ONE

Birchfield wasn't the typical Southern newspaperman. Far from it.

A native New Yorker who used to work at the *Daily News*, he had never even been close to Tennessee before his wife took an accounting job with Sea Ray, the boat company headquartered in Knoxville, a few years back. Living in the South had been an adventure, personally and professionally, but Birchfield relished being the outsider and played it to his advantage whenever possible. He was known for his commanding presence at news conferences, asking questions with that biting Yankee wit. Most people respected him, with some fear and trepidation mixed in.

Billy knew the reporter would be utilizing all his resources on this sordid tale.

"Trey, what do you have for me?" Billy said.

"Good afternoon. I've been spending a lot of time on this Jarvis Thompson story, trying to understand it, and thought we might talk for a minute. It's the biggest story I've had to deal with down here and I want to do it justice as more things unfold. I want to be first and right."

"I can appreciate that. You do what you have to, but you know I can't comment on the record. I'm not sure I should be talking to you at all."

"Mr. Beckett – Billy – I understand you're in a tough position here," Birchfield said. "There are a lot of questions, everything hanging in the balance."

"So ..."

"What I'm wondering now is whether your brother was down in Autumn earlier this month. I think it could have an impact on how this whole thing plays out."

"I'm not following," Billy said.

But he was being followed. He could see in his rear view that the two men in the white car were now close on his tail. He swerved through highway traffic and made an abrupt right turn into a shopping center. The men shot past, the smiling passenger leaning out to mimic a gun with his right hand.

Billy pulled to a stop in the parking lot and scratched his head. *Local yokels? Or something else?*

"I can't say for sure," Birchfield was saying, "but I've gotten to know a source down there who's telling me that some people aren't exactly big fans of Jarvis. When I talked to the guy this morning, he mentioned that your brother had passed through with some woman in a silver car. He was supposedly looking for Charles Ratliff."

Billy hesitated. "So this is all off the record?"

"Totally. I'm just trying to put some pieces together. It could be to your advantage."

"John was in Florida on business last week, but I don't think he got over into the panhandle. If he did, I didn't hear anything about it."

"Maybe not," Birchfield said. "Of course, you hadn't heard about a lot of things. Any dealings with Charles obviously wouldn't be good. Outside of selling drugs and being a deadbeat in general, I don't know what else he's known for. That's what people who are familiar with him say. The fact that cocaine has come up in this thing with Jarvis ... it just seems curious."

Billy scanned the parking lot for the men in the white car. No sign of them.

"John knew Charles a long time ago, and just barely," he said. "He played baseball with Jarvis's older brother, Dante, at Florida State. That's the only connection I know of. I don't think I ever saw Charles at more than a couple of their games."

"Does John still see Dante anymore?"

"Not that I know of," Billy said. "Dante got kicked out of school and went back home. It was a shame, because he was probably good enough to get drafted. John had arm trouble and dropped out not long after. He went back to Sevierville. That's all ancient history."

"Did John have drug issues, too?" Birchfield said. "I know Dante did."

Billy could tell he was being measured by the reporter and was going to play his hand close to the vest for now.

"I'm being completely honest with you, Trey, when I say we don't deal in drugs," he said. "And I guarantee you that Jarvis doesn't either. I think there's more going on here than any of us are aware of."

Silence.

"I don't know you well," Birchfield said, "but I've always heard Jarvis is a stand-up guy, considering all he's had to go through. Our sports writers like him; they say he's friendly enough and a good quote, which makes their lives a little easier. Obviously, he's a hell of a football player. It would be sad if there isn't a better ending than what we have now, but I'll write the story however it presents itself."

"All I'm asking is that you keep an open mind. There may be people with ulterior motives trying to influence things."

"Why would they want to make Jarvis look bad?"

"I don't know at this point."

"And you can't tell me anything more that would help me? Or help *you*?" Birchfield said.

"How about this, Trey. You and I stay in contact, and maybe we can help each other. I'll call you back soon, when I know more."

Billy now had plenty to think about, and his mind was racing as he eased back onto the highway.

Talking to Clarise had been a waste of time. He may have just given her more venom to spew, if that were possible. He already knew she had cozied up to Sonny Bradley. The New Orleans angle was worrisome on several fronts.

Why would John be looking for Charles? And the woman in the silver car?

Billy was starting to let the worst-case scenario, that Jarvis wasn't even alive, feed his fears. No matter what happened down by the river that night, wouldn't he have surfaced by now if he were able?

Maybe John would be talking by the time Billy got back to Knoxville. Of course, that wouldn't fix the damage that had already been done to at least a couple of careers.

At this point, it was all starting to seem like a salvage operation.

CHAPTER THIRTY-TWO

There was a sense of relief in the ICU waiting area when Billy arrived. The doctors expected John to regain consciousness any time and were inside with him now. Pretty soon he'd be able to talk to his family – and the police.

Billy walked up to Rachel and gave her a hug, then put an arm around his father.

"You okay?" he said.

Franklin nodded but was unconvincing. Billy knew the career cop wanted to do something – anything – to help but felt powerless to act. This was out of his hands.

"What did you find out in Florida, son?" Franklin said.

"Nothing for sure, but there are some leads we're working on. Hopefully John is going to help us out here real soon."

A doctor walked into the room, and he was smiling. Finally some good news.

"I think our man is coming around," he said. "You should be able to speak to him soon, if we can get at least a small window of opportunity. We'll have to contact the detective, too, so he can be here."

The legal ramifications would have to be sorted out. At a minimum, John would face charges for cocaine possession, which wasn't going to help his state of mind. And Billy wasn't off the hook either.

For Jarvis, who knew? Each day that passed added to the growing sense of dread.

The doctor returned about a half-hour later and said John was conscious and talking. His family could see him, one at a time.

"You go first, Dad," Billy said.

Franklin was escorted into the back, and Billy sat down beside Rachel. They had run the emotional gamut and knew the ordeal was still far from over. It showed on both of their faces.

"I really appreciate you waiting here with my father," Billy said. "It means a lot to me."

"I didn't know what else to do."

"This will all be over soon and we can get back to normal. I promise."

Rachel registered a look of disbelief. "Normal? We may never see normal again. I don't think you can promise anything at this point."

After ten minutes, Franklin walked out of the ICU, his eyes misty but a smile on his face. "Billy, go see your brother," he said.

John was groggy but seemed aware of his surroundings. His head was bandaged and his face was still swollen and blue.

Billy eased over to the side of the bed, reached out and grasped John's hand. He'd never seen his brother look so utterly helpless.

"Hey buddy, didn't I warn you about hanging out in these rough neighborhoods?" he said. "We've been worried about you. How are you doing?"

John flexed his neck and grimaced. "Not so good," he whispered.

"Do you remember what happened? You and Jarvis were down at the dock."

"No."

"We can't find Jarvis. Did you guys get into a fight or something?"

"The last thing I remember is watching a football game on the boat," John said. "He was with me."

"Was there a problem?"

"No."

"John, the paramedics found cocaine when they treated you on the boat. It was some really pure stuff, and they said you definitely had been using that night. The police also found some in Jarvis's backpack."

John's chest heaved and his eyes welled with tears.

"I'm sorry," he said. "Really sorry."

"Does it have something to do with Charles Ratliff? I heard you were looking for him when you were in Florida last time. You know, Jarvis's father?"

"I don't understand. Charles?"

The pain medication was kicking in again, and John started to fade. A nurse stepped to the bedside to check his vitals.

"You might want to come back later," she said to Billy. He took a long look at his brother, squeezed John's hand and walked away.

Detective Lewis was standing in the waiting room, talking to Franklin when Billy returned.

"How's your brother?" he said.

"Pretty out of it, but I think he'll be okay. I asked him about Jarvis, and he doesn't remember. The meds have knocked him out again, so it'll be a while."

"We really need to know what he knows, whatever it is," Lewis said. "No one close to Jarvis can say what happened. It's all just speculation. I'm going to have one of my men wait here, and hopefully when John wakes back up we can talk to him."

The doctor was standing nearby with a nurse at her station, looking over John's charts.

"Any idea how long he'll be out?" Billy said.

"I would expect most of the night. With these head injuries, it's hard to predict. It's getting late, so why don't you go home and get some rest. Come back in the morning and John should be able to talk some more. He's getting stronger."

Billy went back over to the detective, who was growing noticeably impatient.

"It doesn't sound like we'll hear anything from him tonight," he said. "Can we do this in the morning? I'll meet you here and answer any more questions that might come up."

"That's as long as I'm willing to wait. I've got a lot of people on my ass to figure this out."

The family and the cops weren't the only ones waiting. The national buzz surrounding the case was growing.

When Jarvis resurfaced, *if* he resurfaced, everyone would surely know about it quickly.

CHAPTER THIRTY-THREE

Football is all about crisis management, and Jack Stratton was being forced to learn another hard lesson. The heat was on.

It was bad enough that the coach had only two winning seasons to show for his four at Tennessee, and some of the program's most influential donors were ready to rebuild again. Now Stratton had to address all the off-field questions – his best player going missing, drugs, agents, discipline.

Adding fuel to the fire, just a day before the Alabama game a prominent *Journal* columnist had wondered whether it was time for Stratton to go. The drumbeat had started. Even a monumental win wasn't necessarily going to salvage the season, or the coach's job, especially if Jarvis Thompson wasn't on the field anymore.

The fact that a strong Missouri team was coming to town Saturday, and the Vols desperately needed to keep winning, seemed lost on the fan base, which was still lighting up social media and message boards with conspiracy theories about Jarvis. It was probably lost on most of Stratton's players, too. They were just as preoccupied by the star receiver's disappearance as everyone else, though they weren't saying so publicly.

The coach had put a gag order on them until the weekly media briefing that afternoon, and even then only questions about Saturday's matchup would be addressed. It was sure to be a circus.

Most everyone could agree that Jarvis was an unlikely candidate to be embroiled in such controversy at this stage of his career. He had been a model student in his two-plus years at UT, with respectable grades for a guy who didn't really need a degree, and his community service deeds around Knoxville were exemplary.

Just a few weeks ago, he showed up out of the blue at the children's hospital and spent several hours with the young patients, many of them waging gut-wrenching battles with cancer. He brought a bunch of Vols souvenirs, signed autographs and laughed and played with the kids. The media never even knew.

Whenever the UT coaches needed a high-profile player to get involved in a public-relations project, Jarvis was their man. He was money in the bank with all the university's constituents. They had been fretting for weeks about how much he would be missed next season – a jump to the NFL was a foregone conclusion – and now they were left to ponder this bizarre turn of events.

The coach's place was coming into view, and Billy drove up to the wrought-iron gates and pressed the call button. Stratton was his neighbor, sort of, but at the moment he seemed to be in a world of his own.

The house stood like a white fortress on the bluff, the river on one side and its high stone walls on the other, keeping everyone at bay. A salary of four million dollars a year could buy some serious privacy in Knoxville, and right now that's exactly what the man needed.

Billy was surprised to hear a woman's cheerful voice come over the intercom. It must have been Stratton's wife, Vickie.

"Good morning," she said. "Can I help you?"

"Good morning. This is Billy Beckett. I live down the road here and was hoping I could speak with Coach Stratton. Is he in?"

Vickie seemed less cheerful the second time. "Hold on."

Suddenly Stratton's voice came across, loud and impatient. "Billy, I'm really pressed for time here; I have to be on campus in about an hour. I don't know if we should be talking anyway."

"I won't take much of your time, coach. I promise. This is just between us."

There was a lengthy pause before he heard a couple of clicks, the whir of a motor, and the creaking of the black gates as they slowly began to part. Billy put his Escalade into gear and headed up the long driveway.

Stratton met him before he could even get out of the car.

"Let's go around back," the coach said.

The men took a sidewalk that snaked through a well-attended garden and turned the corner to a gazebo, opening up the most expansive view of the river that Billy had ever seen. This was where the king of Knoxville should live, he thought.

"Beautiful place, coach."

"Not so beautiful when the police are looking for our best player along the river banks. That's what I woke up to this morning. Is there anything new on Jarvis?"

"I don't think so," Billy said. "My brother is conscious but hasn't been able to tell us anything about what happened yet."

Stratton pulled out a couple of chairs from the table and the men sat at his scenic perch. Billy had never been invited to the house, and he certainly wished he weren't here now.

"You know we have the weekly news conference this afternoon," Stratton said. "It won't be a pretty scene. The national media people will be there, just to stir things up, and I don't know what to tell them. At this point, I'm almost speechless. Hell, we're just trying to win football games here."

He took a long look at Billy. "The job just got a whole lot tougher, thanks to you."

"I'm sorry this has fallen on you and the program," Billy said. "Everything with Jarvis was good, you guys beat Alabama and now..."

"And now *you* show up here on my doorstep. If the reporters knew, I'd never hear the end of it."

"I just thought I owed it to you, Jack, to tell you where I'm coming from. I'm a UT guy and I'm trying like crazy to straighten this out so we can all move on. I'm being completely honest when I say that Jarvis and myself had nothing to do with the drugs they found. If my brother is involved, I'll have to deal with that. But Jarvis has just been minding his business, doing what he should be doing. He's a smart kid; you know that."

"What about the money?" Stratton said. "That looks bad, too, especially for you."

"I can't answer that. All I can say is it didn't come from me. My only concern right now is finding Jarvis and getting some answers. I hope we can get him back on the field. You're going to need him down the stretch."

The coach turned away with a pained expression. Billy could tell he was conflicted.

"I'm going to make an announcement to start the news conference today," Stratton said. "Jarvis is suspended indefinitely. It's hard to see how this whole thing will be resolved before the end of the season, so his time here may be over."

"You think he's guilty? Of *what*? I'm wondering if he's even alive."

"Listen, the president is calling the shots on this one; I'm a couple of links down the chain. I just hope Jarvis is well and can get his career back on track, whether it's here or in the NFL. He's a great player, and I know what he's been through to get this far. It's a shame."

Stratton stood and motioned his visitor back toward the front of the house. He had a news conference to attend.

"Billy, I hope this works out," he said. "For all of us."

CHAPTER THIRTY-FOUR

The Knoxville police still had reached no consensus on the case. Assault? Kidnapping? Drowning? Drug deal gone bad? The only sure thing was that the prime suspect, or victim, was missing.

Investigators said there was no evidence to suggest anyone other than John and Jarvis had been down at the dock late that night. Some tire tracks on a gravel service road up near the woods on Billy's property might mean something. Or they could have been left there weeks ago. Police had already searched miles of the riverbanks by boat and found nothing suspicious.

Nothing.

Billy knocked lightly on the door of Matthew Lewis's office and was waved in. The detective, a rumpled man in his early fifties with tired eyes and rapidly graying hair, was on the phone. Billy took a seat beside his cluttered desk.

Lewis was talking to someone who thought they may have seen Jarvis at a flea market over in Oak Ridge, about twenty-five miles to the west. It was the latest of the long shots. He thanked the caller, hung up and rolled his eyes.

"They're coming out of the woodwork," he said. "This big pile of paperwork here, it's all related to the investigation. Most of it isn't worth a thing. I know because I've been sifting through it for a while. Anyway, what do you have for me, Mr. Beckett? I thought we were going to meet at the hospital."

"We're still waiting to see how John is this morning; my father is supposed to call. What I'm wondering is whether you know any more about the cocaine."

"What do you mean?" Lewis said.

"I mean, do you have any idea where it might have originated? You said the other day that it was different than the stuff you normally see around here."

"I can't discuss that with you, Billy. Why would you be interested?"

"I've been talking to some people down in Florida, and they thought maybe it came from there."

"Why there? I keep getting the feeling you know something I should know."

"No, sir, I just have a sense that this case may involve people from there."

"Are you talking about Jarvis's family?"

"Maybe. There are others, too."

"We've already talked to a lot of people. No one seems to know much of anything. Hard to believe this kid just disappeared in the middle of the night."

Billy shifted in his seat.

"You've been doing this a long time, detective," he said. "What does your gut tell you? Doesn't this feel more like a kidnapping?"

"To be honest, I don't know. I'm still looking for motive. Jarvis Thompson is a great football player, but what would holding him accomplish? His family has no money. His value obviously is his future potential in the NFL."

Billy tried to ease the tension just a bit. "Have you seen him play?"

Lewis nodded. "I grew up in Knoxville and my family always had season tickets," he said. "I still get to two or three home games every year. I've never seen a better receiver at UT than Jarvis Thompson. Of course, you've seen him from a different angle."

"Because I'm an agent?"

"Because you're *his* agent, or will be, and you have a lot riding on this. Since he disappeared from your house, one has to wonder exactly how you're involved. I think we've already covered some of that ground. If I recall, you're claiming total ignorance."

Billy was about to mount another defense when the phone rang. It was his father. The doctors said John might be up to talking within the hour. He had been in and out but seemed to be growing more alert.

"I'll be there as soon as I can," Billy said.

He and the detective stood at once. Lewis put on his jacket and grabbed a worn leather satchel that was sitting on his desk.

"They said to give it about an hour," Billy said, "so pick up a sandwich first. Hopefully we'll hear something that will help solve this. I'll see you at the hospital."

CHAPTER THIRTY-FIVE

Rachel's silver Mercedes coupe was sitting in the driveway with the passenger door and trunk lid open when Billy pulled in and dashed into the house.

"Rachel, let's go," he shouted. "I think we may get some answers today. Dad said John is coming around."

There was no response and Billy went upstairs to the master suite. He heard the shower running. A suitcase was open on the bed, partially filled.

Rachel was packing to leave.

Billy knocked on the bathroom door and walked in.

"Where are you going?" he said.

Rachel turned off the water, wrapped a big towel around her and slid open the glass door.

"Back to Charleston," she said. "I talked to my parents again this morning, and they're really worried about me. They want me to come home."

"For how long?"

"I don't know. I just don't like being in the middle of this."

"There you go again, putting yourself in the middle," Billy said. "Why?"

"That's just the way it feels. There's too much going on here, too much attention. This morning I even saw where somebody had posted pictures of me at the hospital on some website. That's sick."

"I just spoke with Dad, and he said John may be ready to talk. We may know what happened to him, what happened to Jarvis. Don't you want to be there?"

"I really hope it works out, Billy. I'll be thinking about you guys."

"*Thinking* about us? Boy, we appreciate that. Sounds like you're not planning to come back."

"It's been on my mind for a while," she said, "really since before all of this happened. I just need to go home and clear my head. My father insisted."

"Is something else going on?"

Rachel closed the bathroom door and slipped into a pair of jeans and a frilly white blouse. She hurriedly applied some makeup and brushed her hair. Apparently, she couldn't get away quick enough.

The news caught Billy completely off guard, like most everything else recently. He sat on the edge of the bed and stared out at the river while he tried to collect his thoughts.

"This is your home," he said. "I thought you were happy here."

"I have been happy, most of the time. I don't know ... I just thought things would be different by now."

"Different how?"

"We don't see as much of each other anymore," she said. "You're always busy, and I seem to be stuck at the office more."

"Stuck? I'm trying to build something that we can both enjoy. It takes a while to get there. I thought you wanted to be part of the business; I know that's what your dad wanted."

"Some days I do. And then there are days like the ones recently. It just seems like everything is falling apart in a hurry."

Rachel's eyes didn't betray any deeper emotions as she kept digging and throwing more clothes into the suitcase. She was in a hurry and still had almost a full closet of her belongings remaining.

"I'll get the rest later," she said, hastily zipping up the case.

"I can't believe you're bailing on me," Billy said.

She reached out and stroked his face; there were no reassuring words. The agent who was always in control was being left to take care of himself.

His famous protégé, the young man who counted on him the most, was missing. His brother was lying in a hospital bed, lucky to be alive. And now Rachel was walking away.

CHAPTER THIRTY-SIX

The secluded cabin was a good place to lay low, but the men were getting stir-crazy. They were out of their element in the rugged mountains of East Tennessee, and the potential for disaster seemed to be growing by the hour.

"What the hell are we going to do with the kid?" said Tommy, the short man. "Every cop in the country is looking for him."

His partner maintained an intense stare, like he was somehow trying to devise a plan. "Mean Gene" was the consummate enforcer, but thinking on his own had never been his strong suit.

"I told you we never should have taken him," he said. "It was a stupid mistake. We don't need extra baggage, especially now."

"You know why we took him," Tommy said.

"Because the boss's kid said so? I think he's lost his mind. This little deal is going to come back to haunt all of us."

Even in crisis, Gene was typically a man of few words. It was unusual for him to be flustered and babbling. But he had been that way since they left New Orleans.

Gene began pacing the floor.

"I tell you, I've seen about enough of these mountains," he said. "Feels like that movie Deliverance or something."

"Deliverance?" Tommy laughed. "You don't exactly come from the big city, Gene."

"I don't care. I think it's time to go home."

Jarvis Thompson sat passively on the couch, his hands and feet shackled. He had no idea why he was kidnapped, who was behind it, what the end game might be.

His right eye was swollen shut from the struggle with the men that night. He had tried to intervene when they attacked John but was no match for professional thugs who were armed and used to taking control of any situation.

There was a reasonable chance he'd be knocked out and thrown in the water. That would have been the end. Instead, Jarvis was led through the woods, beaten, blindfolded and gagged before being shoved in the back of the SUV. The tire iron Tommy was swinging may have broken his right arm. These were old-school criminals.

"I should have killed you right there on the dock," Gene said, leering at his captive. "Hell, I should have killed all of you before now. I could have."

"Just shut up," Tommy said.

"Don't talk to me like that, little man. You know we've got serious problems here. We need to travel, and our baggage is too heavy. More than two hundred pounds too heavy."

"Quit talking about baggage."

Hearing the men argue in panicky tones only ratcheted up the mystery for Jarvis, and the danger. Why was it happening?

Tommy pulled up a chair in front of him and looked Jarvis right in the eye.

"What do you think we should do with you, kid?" he said. "Not that you have a vote."

Jarvis didn't blink. He remained silent.

"You know, Gene, he reminds me of his father. Charles was a man of few words, too. Did you know that we met your father recently?"

That was enough to trigger a response. "Is he the reason you came after me?" Jarvis said.

"That's part of it. He took something that didn't belong to him. Your mother also promised some people that you would do business with them, and she got a cash advance. It all just turned into a big problem. You have some really great parents there."

Tommy laughed, then moved closer with his gun and those wild eyes fixed on his prisoner.

"Our boss doesn't handle disappointment well; it makes him a little angry. And so here we are."

"I don't have anything for you," Jarvis said. "I'm just a poor kid from the projects. A college football player."

"Yeah, and a damn good one. I hear you're going to be a big star in the pros pretty soon. Maybe you'll play for the Saints and we can hang out."

Tommy laid his head back and cackled.

"You'll have lots of cash, but you have some family debts to pay right up front," he said. "I know it may come as a surprise, but you already owe people. And those debts grow in a hurry."

"How can I pay if I don't play? You have to let me go."

"You can barely walk right now, and it looks like I might have broken your arm. Where do you think you'd go, limping around out in the middle of the forest with a broken arm? You just need to stay right where you are. I'm pretty sure you'll get over this, if we don't kill you. The boss just has to figure out how to work things. It's complicated."

Tommy walked to the empty refrigerator for about the fifth time. He opened the door and looked inside, as if something new would magically have appeared.

"I heard on the news that they found some white stuff and cash in your backpack on the boat," he said. "So the cops aren't sure what to think about you right now."

"Cocaine?" Jarvis said. "That's not mine. I didn't have any money either."

"I'm just telling you what I heard. Your friend had some coke on him, too. I guess all that was planted. Now that I think about it, maybe Gene and I did that. We enjoy throwing money and cocaine around. Always makes for a better party."

"What about John?"

"Last I heard he was still feeling the effects of our little visit. I don't guess he's ever been pistol whipped like that before. We almost got carried away, which happens sometimes. He's laid up in some Baptist hospital; he ain't dead. Of course, that could change, too."

Tommy looked over at his partner, who had picked up his handgun and was walking toward the back door.

The look on Gene's face said he was ready to shoot somebody.

The men walked out onto the deck, which was surrounded by the dense vegetation of the national forest.

"We have to finish this, one way or another," Gene said. "Either we let the kid go or we get rid of him. We can't just sit out here in the middle of the Smoky Mountains, the three of us. This is all over the news."

Tommy shook his head. "The boss said to hang tight," he said. "We may have other options."

"What options? Whatever happens, people will be tracking us the rest of our lives."

"Maybe not, if there's a reason for the kid to stay quiet. He has to understand we could come and visit him anytime, anywhere. That's reason enough to keep his mouth shut."

"How the hell is he going to explain where he's been?"

"That's his problem. He's a smart kid."

"I don't like it," Gene said. "I don't like it at all. We're sitting ducks. I'd rather be a moving target."

"Let's be calm and think about it. The boss won't hang us out to dry."

"Maybe not, but his kid would. I don't trust Paul as far as I could throw him. He got us into this. Like I said, there is no plan."

"Just be calm," Tommy said.

The men walked around to the black SUV in the driveway, pulled some more items out of a duffle bag and prepared to stay a while longer. It was a gray day and the light was fading fast in the valley.

"Jarvis, my friend, we're going to stay put until we hear differently," Tommy said. "Mean Gene here is quite the cook, and he's going to make a grocery run so we won't starve to death. No more Vienna sausage and crackers. You just sit tight. We've got this place for as long as we need it."

Jarvis squirmed in his seat and grimaced. "Can you take these cuffs off?" he said. "My arm is really hurting."

"Not a chance. You're a big dude, and I'm guessing you're angry. What I will do is let you watch TV while we're sitting here. Maybe there's a football game on."

Tommy waved his gun in Jarvis's face and laughed again.

"I hope you live to tell your kids about meeting me," he said. "Not everybody does."

CHAPTER THIRTY-SEVEN

Detective Lewis was already talking with John when Billy arrived at the hospital. Franklin Beckett was standing outside his son's room.

"He's much more alert this morning," Franklin said. "I talked to him for a few minutes before the detective came."

"How long has Lewis been in there?" Billy said.

"About fifteen minutes."

"Any idea what John remembers?"

"No, I didn't go there with him. We just talked about how he's feeling. He seemed pretty emotional."

The men took a seat in the waiting area, and after a few minutes the detective walked out. There was a steely look on his face. Billy and his father got up, but Lewis waved them off and hurried down the corridor, disappearing around the corner.

"That's not a good sign," Billy said. "Let me go see what I can find out."

Before he could get to the door, the doctor called his name.

"John has made great progress over the last twenty-four hours," he said. "We've upgraded his condition, and he may even be ready to go home in a few days. I haven't mentioned that to him yet, but you can when you go in to talk to him. That should cheer him up some. He seems pretty depressed."

John was lying in bed and staring at the ceiling as his brother slowly entered the room.

"I hear you're getting better in a hurry," Billy said. "They may let you out of here soon. So what do you remember about that night? Do you know what happened?"

John rolled over on his side and didn't answer. More pieces of his story had been coming together in his head, but he needed to figure it all out before the investigation took some unexpected turn. He couldn't stall the detective, or his brother, much longer.

One thing John knew is that he was lucky to be alive.

Frank Romano didn't have much sympathy for those who failed to deliver, and John could easily have been killed right on the spot. He had heard the tales from Charles the last time he was down in Florida – anyone who dared to cross Romano was as good as dead.

And then what did that crazy addict go and do? Took a cut of the cartel's best stuff and let it get back to the boss. All Charles was supposed to do was deliver the package.

"John, do you know what happened?" Billy said, staring intently into his brother's eyes.

"Most of it is still pretty hazy. I remember sitting there on the boat watching the football game with Jarvis. I got up to go to the bathroom, and when I came back he was out on the dock. I stepped outside ... that's the last thing I remember."

"Were you guys arguing before that?"

"Not really," John said. "He was going on about how great everything will be in the NFL, all the money and women. He was drunker than I've ever seen him, and I just let him go on. No big deal."

"So you don't know who hit you?"

"No. Everything went black after I stepped out onto the deck."

"Well, it looks like Jarvis attacked you for some reason. And if he didn't, who did?"

"The detective was asking me the same thing," John said. "I just don't know. Who would have been roaming around there in the middle of the night?"

Billy sat on the edge of his brother's bed. "What about the cocaine? Did you get it from Jarvis?"

"Why would he give me that? He doesn't even like me."

"The police found some in his backpack, too. Lewis said it looked like the same stuff, so it appears you guys were working together on that," Billy said. "We're all just trying to understand this."

"I really don't want to talk about it any more right now. I'm getting tired."

"This is important, John. Just remember that you have to tell them everything you know. You're already in deep, and it's all going to come out in the end anyway."

John had no response.

"Okay, rest up and let's get you out of here as soon as possible," Billy said. "You can stay with me for awhile and get well. I can use the company."

"Why? Where's Rachel?"

"She decided to go to her parents for a few days. She said she'd be thinking about you."

John rolled back over and closed his eyes. He knew his troubles had only just begun.

CHAPTER THIRTY-EIGHT

The Tennessee mountains were in her rear view as Rachel made her way toward Asheville, North Carolina. It was a straight shot down I-26 from there to the South Carolina coast, and in a few hours she would be standing on the sand at her parents' home on Isle of Palms.

She didn't want to dwell on what she was leaving behind. She was just glad to be moving on, getting away from this growing entanglement with Billy. Would she miss him? Yes, and no. Wasn't that the way Billy had always left women feeling at the end of their relationships? Ambivalent.

"I hope you'll change your mind. Take some time and think about it," said the phone message playing in her ear. "I need you."

There was never much doubt she was needed, right from the start. Billy's business might not have even gotten off the ground without her father on board. The big house, the boat … she was tied to it all.

Living in the relative obscurity of East Tennessee was never Rachel's idea of heaven, but she was young and free and willing to see where it all would lead. She should have known better the first time she set foot in Knoxville.

"It's beautiful, Billy, but there's not a whole lot to do," she said. "I miss the big city already. If I can't have the ocean and shrimp and grits, I want big buildings and nightlife. I like Atlanta."

"How about smaller buildings, a big river and a great college atmosphere?" he said. "We'll find a nice place and I'll hook you up with some real-estate people in town that I know. You can work as much or as little as you like. You're very good at what you do."

She played along. "If your stuff goes as well as you think, I may not work at all. Or maybe I'll just work for you."

"I'm sure I can keep you busy," he said with a devilish grin.

Before long, Rachel was the centerpiece of the Billy Beckett Enterprises entourage.

The North Carolina line was approaching as the phone rang. Rachel figured it was Billy calling again, but there was no ID number and she took it on Bluetooth.

"Hello, Miss King." The man's voice was deep and had a strange accent.

"Yes," she said. "Who's this?"

"We haven't spoken, but I believe we're acquainted. I sent you a little package a while back? A very expensive package."

A chill ran up Rachel's spine. "Package? You must have me confused with someone else."

"I don't think so. You remember Charles, our delivery-man, don't you? You were in the car that day, weren't you?"

"I don't know what you're talking about."

"I believe you do," the man said. "We're still trying to collect on that delivery, Miss King. Can I call you Rachel?"

There was a long pause as she decided whether to hang up.

"You know, this sports agent business, it's hazardous work," the man said. "How is your boyfriend's brother doing anyway? I understand he had a terrible accident down at the river, right there below where you were sleeping. And you never knew a thing. That's your story and you're sticking to it, right?"

"I had nothing to do with what happened to John, or with Jarvis. Where is he?"

"Paul didn't tell you?"

"Paul?" Rachel said. "How do you know Paul?"

"Let's just say he's an old friend, and I know he's very fond of you. You spoke with him that night, didn't you? And the next day, too."

Rachel was speechless.

"Let's be honest," the man said. "You don't care about the football player, and the only reason you care about your boyfriend's brother is that he's been feeding you the white stuff. You know, sometimes it makes you unreasonable. Makes you a little crazy. Have you noticed that?"

"What do you want?"

"I just want to make sure that you put your past behind you. Forget Billy. Don't go back to Knoxville."

Rachel clicked off the call. Her hands were trembling on the steering wheel and she struggled to stay in her lane.

Her mind flashed back to that day in Florida, stopping at that dump of a bar outside Autumn. John went in and a couple of rough characters peered out at her from the door. They weren't there ten minutes, but things hadn't been the same since. It was all a terrible mistake.

And now Paul? Had he been using her all along?

She mashed the gas and headed south.

CHAPTER THIRTY-NINE

It was obvious that Sonny Bradley never knew what hit him.

Authorities recovered the agent's bullet-riddled body from a shallow ditch that runs behind an industrial park out on the western edge of New Orleans. A man had called police after coming across the scene while walking his dog that morning. There wasn't much of an attempt to conceal the murder.

In fact, one of the investigating officers told Mark Fletcher that whoever killed Bradley wanted everybody to know he was dead. Billy was about to find out.

"I've got some news," the private investigator said by phone. "You don't have to worry about your New Orleans friend signing Jarvis Thompson. He won't be signing anybody else."

"Sonny Bradley? What happened?"

"Looks like he lost the big man's support. He's dead. Shot to pieces and dumped, mafia-style. Now we have to wonder why."

Billy shifted uneasily in his office chair.

"This is getting more bizarre by the hour," he said. "What else?"

"Here's what's really interesting," Fletcher said. "Bradley had one of your business cards in his pocket."

"One of *my* cards? I haven't even seen the guy in years. Just the one conversation on the phone."

"I'm guessing that was another little message from Romano. He seems to be taking a serious interest in you. Why is that?"

"I don't know. I was just going about my business until all this craziness started happening. I'm no threat to him, I don't think. Other than Jarvis, I don't know who I have lined up that Sonny Bradley was going all out to recruit."

"I'd be surprised now if Romano isn't behind Jarvis's disappearance," Fletcher said, "but I'm not sure how killing Bradley would help his cause. Unless his cause is just to hurt you."

"Why would Bradley being dead hurt me? Seems like just the opposite. Now there's a bunch of players who need new agents."

"Romano obviously didn't care about that," Fletcher said. "Maybe there's just one player he really cares about."

"Then what good would it do to kidnap Jarvis? This whole thing is only going to knock down his value as a player, if we find him and get him back on the field. Most NFL teams are going to be reluctant to spend a high draft pick on a guy who has been through a sketchy ordeal like this. It doesn't make sense."

"Well, we still don't know what the motivation might be for any of it. But I'll keep digging. I'm guessing the New Orleans cops will be calling you soon about that business card. You're connected, whether you like it or not."

"I'll be expecting it, but there's not much I can tell them. I don't know what's going on," Billy said. "It's about time I found out."

CHAPTER FORTY

The local news played on the television in his hospital room, and John listened intently. The story was changing fast.

UT had suspended wide receiver Jarvis Thompson, who remained missing and was presumably on the run. According to an anonymous source, the player attacked the sports agent's brother in a dispute over drugs. Further, the cocaine found on the boat might be linked to Thompson's family, which had an extensive criminal history in Florida. The agent's brother was improving rapidly and had been moved out of intensive care.

John, in fact, was well enough to sit in a chair. And he was thinking more clearly now, putting more pieces of his story together since his interview with Detective Lewis.

There was a knock at the door, and Billy leaned into the hospital room. The look of disillusionment on his face – like he didn't know who had done the real damage, his protégé or his brother – was unmistakable.

"John, I just heard the news in the car," he said. "Tell me what's going on. I thought you said you didn't remember getting into it with Jarvis. And the cocaine? It all came from him? That can't be true."

John turned his head away, avoiding Billy's steely glare. His voice cracked with emotion.

"It started coming back to me this morning," he said. "I remembered that we were arguing, like we always seem to do, and it got out of hand. I didn't want to be the one to bring him down. I know you have a lot riding on him."

"I don't believe it," Billy said. "I think I'd know if Jarvis was involved in something like this. I've spent a lot of time with him."

"Billy, I'm sorry ... I apologize for my role in it. We just started doing a few lines on the boat and were drinking, and one thing led to another. Once he started talking about what a big star he's going to be in the NFL and all that, I just didn't want to hear it."

"Where is he then?" Billy said. "Do you know that, too? It's been several days now without a word."

"I don't know, but I'm sure he wishes he had grabbed his backpack before he ran. That's going to be a bigger problem for him."

"It's a problem for both of you. Why didn't you tell me you were using again? I could have helped you. Now all of this mess is just thrown out for the whole world to see. It's a killer for business."

"Business?" John said. "Who gives a damn about business?"

Billy turned and walked toward the door. Disillusionment was turning to anger, and John knew that was something his older brother always tried hard to contain.

"*I* give a damn – it's everything I've worked for," Billy said. "I didn't build this thing up to have it blown apart by my own brother. Just because you can't get your pathetic life together doesn't mean I have to put up with it. We're finished."

Billy may have regretted the words as soon as they left his lips, but he didn't turn around. John sat quietly in the chair. He expected to be released soon and hoped they would talk again then.

Maybe cooler heads would prevail. Maybe not.

"I'm going to find Jarvis," Billy said. "Until then, stay out of my way."

CHAPTER FORTY-ONE

The Vols were running through the T and the crowd was cheering, but it was a subdued Saturday at Neyland Stadium. The euphoria of the previous week was long gone.

Countless fans were wearing jerseys and holding signs with the number eleven in a show of support for the missing receiver. Brett Sterling and the other two co-captains walked out for the coin toss arm in arm. It had been a draining week for the team, and for Sterling in particular. He had been quoted in a newspaper story saying Jarvis's disappearance was the "most gut-wrenching loss I've ever experienced. This is real life."

The television announcers had already laid out the whole Jarvis Thompson saga in great detail and turned their attention to the matchup with Missouri. The show must go on, they said, and Tennessee needed to find a way to win without its All-American. Simple as that.

The scene was surreal as Jarvis stared at the screen in the small cabin. He was hungry and dirty and exhausted, but at least the shackles that were digging into his ankles had been removed. His wrists, bloody and raw, remained bound in front of him. His arm ached intensely.

Still, Jarvis had kept his wits about him. His street smarts had always served him well. Even in vulnerable positions, he was looking for a mental edge, whether it was on the football field or just going about his daily life.

Jarvis had gotten a good read on his captors after being holed up together for a week. Mean Gene was intense, fond of playing with his guns, and rarely had much to say that was coherent. The wiry man had a far-away look in his eyes. Tommy, on the other hand, looked like Danny DeVito and never got tired of hearing himself talk. He was a comedian one minute, and then dead serious the next.

Jarvis didn't expect any mercy from either man if it came right down to it.

"Looks like they're going to play without you, kid," Tommy said, fixed for the moment on the television screen. "Which one is taking your place?"

Jarvis continued to stare straight ahead. "Seven," he said.

"Well, Gene, we're pulling for lucky number seven. He'll be my favorite player today."

"Who are we playing?" Gene said.

Tommy laughed and cocked his head in an odd sort of way. "Mississippi, man. Get with the program. We're the guys with the orange T's on their helmets."

The teams kicked off and Jarvis watched intently as Tennessee surrendered a quick touchdown. Another three-and-out by the offense and Missouri had the ball again. The Tigers were favored by a field goal, and the early momentum was with them.

The game didn't hold the attention of either of Jarvis's captors for long. Pretty soon Gene was pacing again with his pistol in his hand and Tommy was chattering away.

"Tell me about your father, kid," he said. "When was the last time you saw him?"

"Been a while. He tries to call me every now and then, but there isn't much to say."

"Was there anything good about him? I mean, did he ever do anything to help you when you were growing up? Take you fishing or anything?"

Jarvis took his eyes off the television. Tommy's sudden interest in a man he had never really known was puzzling.

"He wasn't around much. I don't miss him."

"That's good," Tommy said.

Missouri had moved in front by two touchdowns now, and the Vols had yet to complete a pass to Jarvis's replacement. Coach Stratton was grimacing on the sideline. The crowd was moaning and groaning.

Without the receiver that carried the offense a week earlier, quarterback Stan Holsten was misfiring and the whole team appeared listless and lost.

"You'd be out there if you were smarter," Tommy said. "We wouldn't be sitting here right now."

"What do you mean?"

"You should have gotten rid of that agent friend of yours. He's been holding you back. Still holding you back. Signing with Sonny Bradley would have been the smart move."

"I can't sign with anybody yet, but why would I sign with him? I've never even talked to him."

"Your mother has. I think she had about convinced him that you'd come along. She's not a big fan of Billy either. Apparently there's a lot of people in that boat."

"You don't even know Billy," Jarvis said.

"I just know what I've heard. He's more worried about that big house and his pretty girlfriend than he is about you."

"You're wrong. He's the best friend I've got. I'd probably be dead or in jail if it wasn't for him."

"So look where you are now."

Jarvis turned away.

"What about his brother?" Tommy said. "He's part of the team ... can you trust him?"

"We get along all right. Why?"

"I just wondered why you guys were out there together that night. I don't think he's your friend, kid. The pretty girl isn't either; I know that for a fact."

"And you are?"

"I'm the best friend you got in this house. If it was up to Gene, he'd just shoot you in the back, tell the boss you had tried to escape, and we'd move on to the next thing."

Back on the screen, the Vols fumbled and Missouri pounced on it. The Tigers were already in field-goal range as their offense took the field. This was not Tennessee's day.

"Turn it off," Jarvis said.

The TV went black and the men sat in silence, each apparently immersed in his own dark thoughts. For Jarvis, the chance of getting back on the field was fading fast, and he knew it. He also knew a lot of people had to be looking for him.

SCOTT PRATT

"How long are you going to hold me?" he asked Tommy.

"As long as it takes."

"As long as *what* takes?"

Tommy's phone rang for the second time today, and a smile came over his face as he listened to instructions.

"All right, boss," he said. "Whatever you say. We'll be in touch soon."

"What's the deal?" Gene asked.

"I'm afraid we're going to have to pack up our football hero and take a drive. A long drive. Get the stuff together."

CHAPTER FORTY-TWO

Billy poured himself another whiskey, neat. He was leaning on the bar in his den, alone and deep into a bottle of Jack Daniel's, and his mind was wandering. He usually went easy on the brown liquor, but the job required more tonight. It was time to drift away as soon as possible.

The only interruptions were the calls, mostly from clients who were concerned. Some were surely wavering about upcoming contracts and business commitments, looking for advice, wondering what to do. They needed their agent. Others were probably calling to say goodbye.

Billy didn't answer. He didn't know what to say, and that might have been the strangest development of all.

Rachel still hadn't gotten back to him, but her father sent an email saying he wanted to meet sometime next week. Billy was pretty sure what direction that was headed. Bradley King wasn't the kind of man to sit back and let things happen.

He took another stiff drink and picked up his new Glock pistol from the bar. It was light and easy to use and, like the salesman said, just felt good in your hand.

After just one visit to the practice range, he already felt capable of dealing with most threats that might arise.

As he walked out onto the deck, a cold breeze was blowing and the solitude of the approaching winter pressed in. He still couldn't get his brother out of his head. *Where had he gone wrong with John?* They used to be so tight. Seemed like yesterday they were immersed in the games – football, baseball, basketball. Anything with a ball. Even after the tragic loss of their mother, sports had been their strongest bond. The boys enjoyed each other's company the way only brothers could.

John was almost three years younger, but it didn't matter much. He was the gifted athlete with the old soul, and he could play with anybody.

They both had such ambition, such grand plans for their lives, when Billy headed off to college. It just didn't work out for John. Somehow they lost touch quickly, and things had never been the same.

Now it all had come unraveled. There would be no easy way to reconcile. John was lying to the police and everyone else around him, but why?

Billy flipped the last of the joint into the shrubbery. Some special occasion. He felt worse.

The neighbor's barking dogs shook Billy from his thoughts. Suddenly, motion in front of the house triggered the security floodlights. A sense of urgency came over him.

He walked quickly to the bar, grabbed his gun and headed toward the door. There was a knock. He wasn't thinking clearly; he slid a bullet into the chamber and flipped on the porch light.

Through the beveled glass he could see the distorted silhouette of a large man wearing a dark jacket and cap.

"Who is it?" he demanded. "Jarvis?"

"It's me," came the reply. "John."

Billy swung open the door and stared at his brother, who pulled off the knit cap. His head was still bandaged and swollen. He was wearing green hospital scrubs under the leather jacket.

"What are you doing here?" Billy said. "I know the doctors didn't release you."

"You didn't have to bring a gun to the door. Can I come in?"

Billy thought about it for a few seconds and then opened the door wide. John was unsteady on his feet and wore a confused expression. Both of them were confused.

"I couldn't let things stand where we left them," John said. "We need to talk about that night. And more."

"How did you get here?"

"Dad had left my car in the hospital parking lot. Didn't you notice it missing?"

There was desperation in John's voice, but Billy cut him off.

"I think you need to go," he said. "There's nothing to be gained here. Not now."

"Please ..."

"Do you understand the damage you've done? And we still don't know the full extent yet."

"I want to help make things right."

"How?" Billy said. "You told the cops that Jarvis assaulted you and ran. And the drugs and the cash ... how can you make anything right? This is a full-blown disaster."

"Just hear me out."

The story unfolded.

John hadn't had time to react that night by the river. He and Jarvis were on the dock drinking and listening to music. A football game from the West Coast was on the television on the boat, and John had stopped to catch the score before ducking into the bathroom for another quick line. He heard a strange voice outside the window, where Jarvis was still standing on the dock. He walked out.

The next thing John knew, doctors were staring into his eyes. He was a lucky man, though he didn't feel like it now.

"I think I know who took Jarvis," he said.

Billy was taken aback. "Who?"

"It's some guys from New Orleans, mafia guys. They were sent here to cause trouble for all of us. Especially you."

Billy looked his brother straight in the eye.

"How do you know this, John? Tell me!"

John fell into a chair, ran his fingers through his hair and stared at the floor. His eyes filled with tears.

"They wanted me to help them," he said.

"Help them *how*? Tell me, John!"

"The cocaine. They gave it to me, a small package of pure stuff, down in Florida. They told me to make sure Jarvis doesn't sign with you; I wouldn't owe them anything if he didn't. I knew he wouldn't let you down, no matter what I did, but I took it anyway. It was so much ... I couldn't help myself."

"And Charles was there, and you were with Rachel?"

"She didn't know what it was about ... she waited in the car."

Billy closed his eyes for a few seconds and tried to make sense of this.

"Then you come back and plant some of that shit in Jarvis's backpack that night."

"No, I didn't. I swear," John said. "Those guys must have done it before they left and took Jarvis with them. The money, too."

"So you took their drugs to betray me. And now Frank Romano's hoodlums have Jarvis stashed away somewhere. You've brought all these people into our lives. It's unbelievable. Are you trying to ruin me? Everything I've built ... I took you in and tried to help you. I've always tried to help you."

Billy was becoming more enraged by the minute. He towered over his brother, who was slumped in the chair, and pulled him up by the jacket lapel until they were almost nose-to-nose.

"You have to tell the police," he said. "Right now."

"I can't," John sobbed. "They'll kill me. And they'll kill Jarvis, too. I don't think there's any doubt."

Billy stepped back and took a deep breath. He headed over to the bar and picked up his Glock again.

"I may kill you right now," he said. "You better leave while you have a chance."

John stumbled to the porch and turned to say something else, but the door slammed in his face. Billy went back to the bar and poured another whiskey. His hands were trembling.

Forget calm, steady and focused. He was seething. There would be hell to pay for this.

CHAPTER FORTY-THREE

Dawn was breaking and a gorgeous sunrise was about to light up the sky when Billy opened his eyes. A light fog had begun to lift from the valley, if not from his throbbing head.

He was still sitting in his favorite chair. The whiskey glass beside him on the table had one last swallow to offer, and he emptied it before getting up to find his cellphone. It had been left outside on the veranda.

Billy didn't bother to scroll through a new batch of messages, instead tapping the number for Mark Fletcher. When he didn't get an answer, he left a message of his own.

"I'm coming down," he said, "as soon as I can get a flight out of here. I'll let you know."

Within a minute, the phone rang.

"Kind of early, isn't it? It's still dark here," Fletcher said. "What's up in Tennessee, besides you?"

"There's plenty more that we need to talk about," Billy said. "Things have changed."

"So you know something new?"

"Yeah, and it looks like we were right about the New Orleans connection. I'll tell you when I get down there."

"Did you get the message I left you last night?" Fletcher said.

"No, but I've got a bunch that I haven't heard yet. What did you say?"

"I mentioned that I had learned a little bit more about Romano. You'll find it interesting. Just let me know when you fly in and I'll pick you up."

Billy sat down at his computer and made a reservation for the ten o'clock Delta flight – Knoxville to Atlanta to New Orleans. He'd have to move fast to make it, but that would put him in the Big Easy about two o'clock Central time. He texted the info to Fletcher and prepared to pack a light travel bag.

After more than a week, Billy had to believe Jarvis wasn't being held in the Knoxville area, if he ever was to begin with. He'd be hidden somewhere along the Gulf Coast. Somewhere near Romano and his men.

Billy had to find out for himself.

On his way out the driveway, he grabbed the newspaper from the box and took a quick glance at the front. A story written by Trey Birchfield was bannered across the top. It said investigators now thought Jarvis's disappearance may be a kidnapping linked to mob activity, which would confirm John's latest account. So that much must be true.

Birchfield's story didn't name sources, and there was no specific mention of Frank Romano and his organization. Reporters were obviously on the trail.

Billy was tempted to go to Detective Lewis and tell him everything he knew, but he was afraid that would blow up in his face. There were already too many leaks out there. Romano would see it coming, Billy thought, and Jarvis might never be heard from again. Too much at stake.

Billy maneuvered his silver Escalade along the winding neighborhood roads and toward Interstate 140. It was about a thirty-minute drive to the airport out in Alcoa during the morning rush hour, and he decided to make a couple of calls on the way.

"Good morning, Trey," he said. "I read the story in the *Journal* this morning. Interesting. How did that come about?"

Birchfield seemed to be caught a bit by surprise.

"Just reporting the thinking behind the scenes," he said. "The cops haven't been able to piece together any kind of local angle that makes sense. Do you have something to add?"

"I noticed Romano's organization wasn't named."

"They're not willing to go that far yet. But you can read between the lines."

"You said you had a friend at the New Orleans paper," Billy said. "Did you ever talk to him about what we discussed?"

"We talked, but he didn't say much. He thought it was plausible that Romano's gang could be involved somehow but hadn't seen or heard any evidence of it yet."

"What about Sonny Bradley's murder?"

"It's still under investigation. The guy was tied up in so many crooked deals, anybody could have wanted him dead. He didn't have a lot of friends."

"Yeah, but the fact is that he was controlled by Romano," Billy said. "That connection isn't going away."

"I know the detectives have talked to Romano a couple of times. Nothing has stuck; he's a Teflon guy with a lot of loyal people around him. Do you know something I haven't heard?"

"I'm going down to New Orleans this afternoon and will know more. I told you we might help each other on this. Why don't we meet when I get back?"

"I'll be waiting to hear," Birchfield said. "Good luck."

Billy was nearing his exit as he looked down at his phone again. His fingers instinctively went to the top of his favorites list. After several rings, Rachel's greeting came on and the phone kicked to voice mail.

"Good morning," he said. "I know it's early, but it's been a couple of days and I was hoping we could talk. Please call me."

Billy wasn't sure where to start with that conversation, or how it might end, but he was anxious to have it.

CHAPTER FORTY-FOUR

Rachel called just as Billy arrived at his gate. Passengers were stirring in preparation for boarding, and he walked across the hallway to a quiet area to talk.

"I've got some bad news about John," he said.

"Oh, no," Rachel said. "He's gotten worse?"

"No, I'd say he's about to be released, if he hasn't been already."

"You don't know?"

"He walked out of the hospital and came to the house last night."

"Why?"

"He wanted to tell me the truth about what happened."

Silence.

"He admitted that the cocaine came from Romano," Billy said, "and he was supposed to be helping them."

"Helping them how?" Rachel said.

"With Jarvis. They wanted to get him away from me and over to Sonny Bradley. When it wasn't going like they planned, Romano apparently sent somebody up here for a visit. I don't know if it was one guy or more. They had been watching my place, I guess, and it just happened that John and Jarvis were alone together that night."

"So they have Jarvis?" she said.

"It's the only thing that makes sense, if he's still alive. I'm getting ready to fly to New Orleans and see Mark Fletcher. Hopefully we'll turn up something down there that will break this open."

"Surely the police are all over this. Shouldn't you go to Detective Lewis and tell him your story?"

"I'm not ready yet. I need to be sure about some things first. We can't afford any mistakes."

Billy checked his watch and looked out the big window as another jet touched down on the runway.

"Let me ask you," he said. "Does any of this surprise you?"

"What do you mean?" Rachel said. "It's all a surprise to me."

"Weren't you the woman in the silver car?"

"What?"

Billy saw the Delta attendant across the way swing open the door to his gate and walk to the podium to make the first boarding announcement. Many of the passengers stood and started collecting their carry-ons for the short flight to Atlanta.

"I have to go," he said, "but I need to know more about this. I'd rather talk face to face. I don't suppose you're planning to come back here in the next few days?"

"No, Billy."

"All right, I'll come see *you*."

"Wait, that won't —"

Billy clicked off the call, picked up his belongings and walked toward the jetway door.

CHAPTER FORTY-FIVE

The bag of cocaine was starting to dwindle after a week on the road, and so was the resolve of the men who had been beating the bushes for Jarvis Thompson.

Dante had run into one dead end after another on their loop from Florida to Tennessee and back. They had left Autumn that morning, heading west after one last conversation with his mother. Clarise said she hadn't heard anything more about her youngest son, and her mind was even more scattered than usual. After the murder of Sonny Bradley, she was sure Jarvis was dead, too.

"No one is safe," she told Dante. "What if they come for me?"

"Why would they want *you*?" he said.

"Because I took their money."

"That was an investment that didn't pay off. You're not worth anything now; Jarvis is the only one in the family that is. If they have him, they don't need you."

Dante and his friends were a rough-looking threesome to start with. A week on the road hadn't helped. They had been sleeping in an old brown van that Dante had stolen in Panama City, scraping by on fast food and cheap liquor while hopscotching around aimlessly. They were traveling with little more than a few belongings in a backpack.

Once their powdery fuel was finished, there wasn't going to be much left to keep T.J. and Isaac in the game.

"Seventy-five miles to New Orleans," Dante announced from behind the wheel as the van passed through Gulfport, Mississippi on I-10.

T.J. stared blankly at the interstate traffic from the passenger seat. "And then what?"

"I got a couple of ideas."

"I hope they're better than the ones you've had so far, bro," Isaac said from behind. "This back seat is getting old. Real old."

"You have a better plan?" Dante said.

"All I know is we've been riding around for a week, and now we're headed the opposite way of home. Seems like we're just chasing a ghost."

"Here's what we know for sure," T.J. said. "Jarvis is missing, and there's a good chance he's dead. The guy in New Orleans who wanted to be his agent is dead. And now we're going to New Orleans."

"I been thinking," Isaac said. "It looks like we're dealing with the mob here. If they have Jarvis and find out we're looking for him, these assault rifles ain't gonna be enough."

"There wouldn't be that many men around him. It draws too much attention. If we can find out where he is, there'll be a way to get him back. I believe that."

T.J. reloaded the cocaine bullet and offered it to Dante. "Still holding off?" Dante nodded and T.J.

inhaled an eye-watering hit before passing it to his friend in the back.

"You gotta do what you gotta do," T.J. said. "This is a family thing for you. Me and Isaac owed you, but I think we're about even now. We don't need to die for no good reason."

"When did you boys start worrying about dying?"

"Since we heard about that agent, rotting in some ditch, full of holes. That's the same damn people we're supposed to take down. Right?"

"I don't like it," Isaac said, growing more adamant. "You can't give me enough blow to make me think we're in a good situation here. We're just walking into big-time trouble."

"So you want to go home?" Dante said. They both nodded.

The van had crossed into Louisiana, and Dante drove on in silence until a rest area came into view. He flipped on his turn signal and exited.

"What are you doing?" T.J. said.

Dante stopped in a parking spot but left the engine running.

"Get your stuff, and take that baggie with you. Maybe that'll get you a ride home with some trucker. I'm going to New Orleans."

"So you're just going to leave us out here on the interstate?" Isaac said. There was no answer.

The men looked at each other and thought it over. They slowly piled out.

The side door slammed, and the van rumbled away.

CHAPTER FORTY-SIX

Mark Fletcher's juices were flowing again when he pulled to the curb at New Orleans International Airport.

He had spent twenty-five years as a detective with the Atlanta Police Department and never feared the high-profile cases. They were, in fact, the most attractive part of the job.

Overseeing security details and background checks for NFL teams was mundane by comparison, but the offer from the Falcons had been too good to pass up, so Fletcher became immersed in the strange culture of professional football. The rush of police work was addictive, though, and he missed it. And sometimes his past and present intersected in unusual ways.

It had been a while since a case had intrigued him like this one.

Billy barely broke stride as he approached the white Lexus sedan and tossed his laptop and carry-on bag in the back seat. He opened the passenger door and leaned in with a smile and firm handshake.

"It's about time I saw that pretty face again," he said.

Fletcher was a man of about sixty, a native Texan with long silvery hair and a tan complexion. He had a casual elegance about him and was remarkably stylish, unusual qualities for an ex-cop. Billy always admired the way he went about his business.

Years of working in the NFL had given Fletcher a good feel for New Orleans and its gritty DNA. He knew his way around town and how to deal with the locals.

"Good to see you, too, but sorry about the circumstances," he said in that distinctive Texas English, which sounded like a Southern accent with a twist. "Let's see if we can't get to the bottom of this mess."

Fletcher put the car in gear and ducked into the flow of traffic away from the airport. They were headed for a Marriott about ten miles outside of town, just off the grid but still close enough to the action.

"Yeah, I'm afraid things haven't gotten any better since this all started," Billy said. "I just found out last night that my brother is mixed up in it somehow. Romano's guys had given him the cocaine the cops found on him."

"What does that mean?"

"It was incentive for him to help them. Powerful incentive apparently. They wanted to get Jarvis away from me, into Sonny Bradley's clutches, and were willing to do anything that might make a difference. They knew John had the habit and was vulnerable."

"But it wasn't working," Fletcher said.

"Right, and I guess that's why they came to my house that night. I don't know what the plan was, but apparently it went all to hell. They end up nearly killing John and taking Jarvis. I'm guessing they brought him back here, somewhere."

Fletcher shook his head in amazement.

"That's an incredible story," he said. "I don't remember a big-time college athlete ever being kidnapped like that. A lot of people know what Jarvis looks like, especially now, so he'd be hard to hide for long."

"I don't understand the end game," Billy said, "and that's always a problem."

"Listen, I'm sorry to hear about your brother."

"Well, he's going to be all right, at least physically. I may never speak to him again, but I can't worry about that now. We just have to find Jarvis. It's driving me crazy to think he's out there and I'm not able to do anything to help him. That's why I'm here."

"What makes you think he's still alive? Romano's guys could have panicked and killed him. Hell, they could have tossed him in the river and nobody knows it yet."

"I thought you were the positive thinker," Billy said with a slight grin. "I just have a feeling. Jarvis is tough, and it wouldn't end like that."

"So why didn't you just go to the cops in Knoxville?"

"I still might, but a lot of it is speculation right now. I want to take a day or two to digest what John told me and see what transpires down here. I'm still trying to understand how kidnapping Jarvis helps Romano's cause. What's the motive? If the kid isn't playing football, making lots of money, what good is he to their operation?"

Fletcher thought about it for a few seconds and pursed his lips. He had seen all sorts of crimes through the years, from all sorts of angles, and knew motivation was a hard thing to rationalize. Crazy people do crazy things.

"Maybe he's just a pawn," Fletcher said. "A very prominent pawn for sure, but just a piece in a bigger game."

"What do you mean?"

"Remember, I said I'd learned something about Romano. About his son, actually."

"His son?"

"Yeah, Paul Romano. He was supposedly being groomed to take over the family business one day. I heard he's nuts, too, but in a different sort of way. Well, he had a falling out with his father a couple of years ago and decided he was going off to be a musician, of all things. He tried to put all the mob stuff down here behind him."

"Where is he now?" Billy said.

"From what I understand, he's in South Carolina. In Charleston."

"That's interesting. Do we know what he's into these days?"

"Not exactly, but he had been playing in some local band there. I don't think it amounted to much. The people I talked to said he was struggling and may be drifting back toward his father. They've been seen together a few times lately."

Billy looked puzzled.

"So how does the son fit into all of this? Is there some link to Jarvis?"

"That remains to be seen," Fletcher said, "but it's worth thinking about. He's another player on the board. Do you have a certain way you want to come at this?"

Billy took a minute to collect his thoughts.

"Somebody down here knows where Jarvis is," he said. "That's where everything starts. We have to tap into that network somehow and get some answers. And we need to do it fast. The longer this goes on, the less chance we'll see him again."

"I just haven't gotten very far yet with the people I know. The New Orleans underbelly is different; it's more guarded than some other places. Sometimes it takes a few days. Do you have any contacts here?"

"Not really, but there are some players who were clients of Sonny Bradley's. I know Dexter Early, the Saints linebacker, was one, and I think the Johnson kid who plays for the Pelicans. I'll see if they'll talk to me. They're going to need a new agent anyway."

"That means Romano will know you're in town pretty soon, if he doesn't already. It doesn't take long for word to travel here."

"That's good," Billy said. "By the way, do you have an extra gun?"

The old detective raised an eyebrow.

"Of course. But we don't need guys like you getting involved in gun play down here. I know your dad's a cop, but I thought you were a lover, not a fighter."

Billy smiled. "I've always been a fighter. This is just a different kind of fight."

An intense look came over Fletcher's face as he drove. He finally had another mission he could sink his teeth into.

CHAPTER FORTY-SEVEN

Billy laid back on the hotel bed and started scrolling down the screen. Two dozen calls from clients alone. He either needed to start answering the phone or quit looking at it.

A burning sensation roiled his gut; he could feel his business slipping away. The cardinal rule – there had to be constant contact – had been broken and now he was forced to play catch-up and manage the damage on the fly. That never worked for long.

He wished Rachel were still around to help soothe hard feelings. She was always good at that.

Most of his clients, Billy figured, wouldn't be scared off by all the bad publicity. Not yet anyway. The mutual trust they had built would hold things together, and the players would just go about their business until they knew more. There were far more important things than agents to worry about late in the NFL season.

At the same time, even an indirect connection to kidnappings and cocaine and payoffs could damage reputations and spread like wildfire. None of the players needed that taint. If one or two of Billy's more prominent clients got antsy and decided to leave, others would likely follow. To some, changing agents wouldn't be a big deal. Happened all the time.

Billy wanted to hear from Marvin Buckles. The Dolphins defensive end was one of his first clients, a free-spirited Oklahoman who was unfailingly upbeat. He stayed in contact with several of Billy's other clients and would be the best barometer of their current mindset.

"Marvin, I'm sorry I've been out of touch, but I'm running around and trying to figure out what the hell is going on here, and it's just taking more time than I thought," Billy gushed over the phone.

"Slow down there, man, I know you've been busy. I heard your brother is better, which is good. Anything new to report on Jarvis?"

"No, but I'm down in New Orleans working on some things. I just didn't want you to think I'd forgotten."

"Forgotten what?"

"Forgotten everything. I just haven't been myself lately."

"I've talked to several of these guys ... we've been try-ing to follow the news," Buckles said. "Sounds like a big mess. We're all worried about you."

Billy's eyes suddenly grew moist and his voice cracked with emotion.

"Listen, don't worry about me," he said. "You worry about *you*, having a strong finish to the season. You know I'll be right there fighting to get you everything you deserve when it's over."

"We're tight, Billy, and I appreciate everything you've done for me. But I have to be straight with you. Some of the younger guys may be easier to convince to try something new. There are a lot of agents out there, and some of them are like vultures. When they see trouble like this ..."

"I'll be talking to all of my guys, starting with you," Billy said. "This isn't what it appears to be, trust me. Just hang with me, Marvin, and enjoy that Miami sunshine. I'll see you soon."

There was a knock at the door as the conversation ended. Billy saw Fletcher through the peephole and let him in, then scanned the hallway in both directions. A new reflex.

"I've got those cell numbers you wanted," Fletcher said. "I don't know how easy it'll be to run these guys down on the spur of the moment. The Pelicans are on a road trip, but the Saints are playing here Sunday, so Early is probably around town."

Dexter Early was a local product, a linebacker from nearby Metairie, on the south shore of Lake Pontchartrain. He had gone to school at LSU and was easy pickings for an agent like Sonny Bradley, who exploited his roots in the talent-rich area to full advantage.

As far as Billy knew, Early hadn't decided yet to sign with anybody else and might be willing to meet with him. They had talked once right after the player left college, but nothing came of it. Bradley swooped in and added another workhorse to his growing stable.

Billy tried the number as Fletcher took a seat.

"Hello, is this Dexter?"

"Who wants to know?"

"This is Billy Beckett. I'm a player agent and we spoke a couple of years ago when you were coming out. I thought we were pretty close on a deal then."

Early didn't seem to have much patience for this conversation.

"I'm really busy, man," he said. "What do you want?"

"I'm in town and just thought I'd see if you had new representation. It's really unfortunate what happened to Sonny."

"Yes it is."

"So what now for you?"

"I haven't decided yet," Early said. "There's a guy who was working with Sonny, Blaine Eldridge, who has picked up some of his clients. But I'm not worrying about it until after the season. We're still trying to win football games here."

"I know it's been a tough year for the team, but I understand you're having your best season. I always thought you were a great player, going back to those games against my Vols. Y'all didn't show us much mercy. You were a beast in that defense."

Early seemed to be warming up. "I remember now. You're from Tennessee."

"Yeah, but don't hold that against me," Billy said. "I represent several SEC guys and take a lot of pride in it. We like diversity in the family, and you'd fit right in. I'd love to talk to you about your future."

"I don't know if I have time right now," Early said. "Maybe later."

"Well, I'm out here at the Marriott at Lakeway, in your old neighborhood, and I won't be around long. Could we get together later today?"

Early took a deep breath. It sounded like he was giving it some thought.

"We practiced this morning, so I might be free after a while," he said. "I was going to see my momma this evening. Maybe on the way."

"Why don't you stop by and we'll chat? Wouldn't take an hour. Better yet, why don't you just come about six and I'll buy you a steak at Ruth's Chris? Then you can go see your momma. She won't have to cook for you."

"Ruth's Chris? Hmmm. Fair enough, man. I'll meet you there at six."

Fletcher nodded approvingly from across the room.

"Nice touch," he said. "If I was a young stud looking for an agent, I'd hire you."

"That's good to hear," Billy said, "but right now I need to make sure I keep the clients I already have. So you think word will get back to Romano's people that I'm here?"

"Yeah, I'm thinking they're already pretty tuned in to your whereabouts. You're going to be on a lot of people's radar as long as Jarvis is missing. Early may even lead them your way without knowing it. We need to be prepared for anything."

"I need a rental car," Billy said. "You can drop me at Hertz in a couple hours and I'll drive on over to the restaurant. I'll meet you back here later. In the meantime, why don't you see what you can find out about this Blaine Eldridge. It wouldn't hurt to know a little more about him."

CHAPTER FORTY-EIGHT

Dexter Early couldn't promise anything, but the meal was excellent and the meeting seemed productive. Time would tell.

The linebacker had given Billy some insight into Sonny Bradley's operation, which was now somebody else's operation. It was a sham, Early thought. After a couple of beers, he readily admitted that things hadn't gone well from the start.

"Dude was always distracted," he said. "Never really seemed all that interested in my career. Some of the other guys felt that way, too, but he kept adding new players to the roster. Don't get me wrong; I hate what happened to him. But he wasn't much of an agent. I don't think he even liked sports."

"Why did you sign with him?" Billy said.

"He was local, a flashy guy, and made a lot of big promises about what he would do for me. I just wanted to play in the NFL; it was all I cared about. Young and foolish, I guess."

Billy wondered if the linebacker had any idea that Bradley was in danger.

"It's pretty easy to put yourself in danger in New Orleans if you're not careful," Early said. "Sonny seemed to have some scary people around him, so it's not that big of a surprise."

"What's the word down here on who may be behind it?"

"I'm not going there, man. I'm a football player. I'm just trying to do my job, get through the rest of the season in good shape and move on. The police can worry about that stuff."

Billy asked him if he'd heard about the Jarvis Thompson case. Early said he had followed developments and was perplexed like everyone else.

Without mentioning their relationship, Billy said he had read that the receiver's disappearance was linked to "criminal elements" and asked Early what he thought about that.

"There's a lot of craziness in this world," he said. "I grew up in the middle of it, and it sounds like Jarvis Thompson did, too. It tends to follow you."

Billy pondered that as they walked out of the steakhouse, shook hands and parted company. He was distracted enough that he had to stop and think about what kind of rental car he was driving and where he had left it. He located the silver Altima in the rear parking lot.

It was only a couple of miles back to the hotel, and Billy was interested to see if Fletcher had found out anything new from his contacts.

Just as he put the key in the ignition, he noticed a black SUV had boxed him in. It was idling with its running lights on. A minute passed before he stepped out and approached the driver's window. The glass slid down.

"Excuse me, but I need to get out," Billy said.

From the darkness, he could make out the barrel of a handgun pointed at this face. His heart fluttered. Obviously, it hadn't taken Romano's men very long to find him.

"I have another idea," the driver said. "Get in."

A passenger door opened and another armed man in the back waved Billy toward him. He slowly slid into the vehicle and the doors locked as the driver sped away.

"I'm sure this is a misunderstanding, gentlemen," Billy said, trying to keep his cool. "I'm not anybody rich or famous, or even important. I don't want any trouble."

"Nobody does," the man beside him said. "Just be quiet, Mr. Beckett."

The driver headed back in the direction of the airport on Interstate 10 before taking an exit south. Five minutes later, the SUV was on a winding state route along the Mississippi River.

Billy's pulse quickened as they slowed on a long straightaway. There were just a few points of light and no approaching vehicles in the area, which appeared to be an old industrial park.

"Pull into this lot," the man in the back said. "Go that way, toward the river."

The driver went to the far edge of the property and stopped. He turned off the engine and for a few moments the three men sat quietly in the dark, preparing for something to happen. Billy was afraid to know exactly what.

Finally, the one in the back turned to him.

"We've been watching you," the man said, rubbing the barrel of his revolver along the agent's jawline, "and we don't like what we've seen. Gene here had you in his crosshairs once up in Tennessee. Could have been the end right there."

Billy could feel his scalp tingle, but he didn't flinch. "What have I done to *you*?"

"It's not me. And it's not Gene."

"Who then?"

Silence again.

"So why are you here in lovely New Orleans?" the man said. "I know it's not just to wine-and-dine Sonny Bradley's clients. Shame about Sonny, wasn't it?"

"I'm looking for someone you might know. Jarvis Thompson. Where is he?"

The man cackled.

"Would you like for that to be the last thing you ever hear?" he said.

"While we're at it, I'd also like to know why you came after him. We were all just going along, minding our own business."

"Funny how one man's business can affect another's. We got a job to do, like anybody else. Our jobs just tend to get a little messier. Unfortunately for you, this one is probably going to end that way, too."

The man moved close to Billy. "Now open that door and let's slide out."

CHAPTER FORTY-NINE

A stretch of dense woods hugged the river bank, just a few yards from where the car was parked, and getting there in a hurry was Billy's only thought. His athleticism was about to be tested in ways he could never have imagined.

As the door opened, he uncoiled with a backhanded blow to the man's forearm. There was a groan and the gun fell to the floorboard. Billy rolled out and hit the ground running before either man could react.

For several frantic minutes he dashed blindly through the trees. The branches ripped at the flesh on his face and hands, but he kept going. He just hoped he wouldn't end up in the water.

Finally, he stopped and crouched in the cold brush. He could feel the blood rushing through his body, pulsing from head to toe. No one was behind him, it seemed, but the men were still dangerously close. He strained to hear.

A maniacal laugh filtered through the trees, and then that voice again.

"C'mon back, Mr. Beckett," the man called out. "You got the wrong idea; we're not going to hurt you.

SCOTT PRATT

And we're damn sure not going to chase you through the woods. It's dark and I don't even have on my running shoes."

Billy wasn't sure what to make of this. Were Romano's thugs supposed to kill him, or just lead him to believe that? The threat was certainly real enough.

After a couple of minutes, he heard the SUV start and ease away from the woods. He waited. Convinced he was now alone, he continued along the riverbank until he came to a clearing in the trees. The mighty Mississippi, which snakes down all the way from Minnesota to New Orleans before emptying in the Gulf of Mexico, was just to his left.

Billy patted his chest. Fortunately his cell phone had managed to stay tucked in the inside pocket of his jacket. He pulled it out and called Fletcher.

"Mark, I've run into a little problem," he said.

"Where the hell are you?"

"I don't know, but I'm pretty sure Romano knows I'm here."

"What can I do now?" Fletcher said.

"Get in the car and go toward the airport on I-10. You'll take one of the last exits just before you get there, maybe Williams Parkway, and go south toward the river. I'm somewhere in that area, near an old plant. If you haven't heard from me yet, just pull over and wait. I'm still on the move."

"Are you all right?"

"Just a little cold and wet. Otherwise okay."

"I'm heading to the car now," Fletcher said. "Let me know."

Billy tried to get his bearings on a cloudy, dark night. He didn't want to run into Romano's men again, so he continued along the river for several more minutes before climbing a small ridge and scouting out his surroundings.

He could see highway lights at the other end of a wide swath of land and started walking in that direction. The occasional car passed, and Billy thought about trying to flag one down and catch a ride. Too risky, he decided.

He stayed well off the shoulder of the road until he came to a highway marker. Billy pulled out his phone again.

"I'm on Highway 48. Not sure exactly where."

"I'm getting close," Fletcher said. "I'll turn on my flashers and go slow. Call me when you see me go by."

Billy moved off to the side again, and within five minutes he noticed the flashing lights coming around the bend. The white car passed.

"Right here."

Fletcher found a place to turn around while Billy stood at the roadside. Shivering, he jumped in the car and took a deep breath before pulling off his jacket and shoes.

"There's another jacket in the back," Fletcher said. "You don't look so good."

"This isn't quite the evening I had planned, but now there's no doubt in my mind that we're on the right track."

"Why is that?"

"Two guys with guns pulled up in the restaurant parking lot and forced me into their car," Billy said.

"Maybe the same two who kidnapped Jarvis. I'm lucky to be sitting here."

"Why don't we just go to the cops?"

"These guys will kill Jarvis before they can get to him; I'm convinced of that, too. They wouldn't think twice. Seems to me that there's a very casual air of danger about all of this."

"Casual air of danger. I'll have to remember that one."

Fletcher gave the Lexus the gas. "They may be waiting for you at the hotel," he said.

"No, they won't try this twice in one night. Just take me back to the restaurant so I can get my car. I'll meet you at the hotel, in the bar. I need a drink."

CHAPTER FIFTY

Fletcher was sitting at a back table and starting on his second Scotch and water when Billy ambled into the Gilded Tiger.

A shower and change of clothes had done him good, but he still looked like a fighter who had just lost by a knockout. The cocktail waitress walked up with an uneasy smile as he pulled out a chair.

"Jack Daniel's, neat. And make it a double."

The waitress jotted down the order on her little napkin and giggled. Billy turned to Fletcher and shrugged.

"Interesting night," he said. "And what a week."

"In case there was any doubt, these guys are about as brazen as it gets. That's a tradition of criminals in these parts. They like to flaunt their badness."

"If you're going to go and kidnap famous people, you have to be pretty damn crazy."

"Or fearless," Fletcher said. "If we're talking about Romano, he's not thinking about consequences. That's not the way his mind works."

"But what's the payoff? If he wanted me out of the way, his thugs could have killed me tonight. One of them said they already had me in their sights back home."

"Maybe that's where things were headed."

"It's almost like they're toying with me," Billy said, "and I still don't understand why. But it's about to stop. I promise you that."

Fletcher leaned back in his seat and studied his friend. The calm, deliberate sports agent he knew was rattled. He was being forced to play a different kind of game, and his temper could easily spiral out of control. He surely didn't need a weapon in his hands to make things worse.

"What did you find out about Blaine Eldridge?" Billy said.

"Turns out he's another lawyer who spends a lot of time defending the mob's rank-and-file lowlifes who get in trouble. There's nothing special about him; he's a lot like Bradley. The biggest difference is Eldridge isn't from around here, so he doesn't have the lifelong connections. That makes him stand out."

"Where's he from?"

"I know this sounds strange, but South Carolina. Charleston. He came here about a year ago and started helping Bradley with the management firm."

Billy rubbed his chin. "Charleston? That city is getting more popular all the time. Wonder if Eldridge knows Paul Romano?"

"I'd say there's a very good chance."

"I also have to wonder if Rachel has ever run across either of them. She knows a lot of people there. That's something I'll ask her. Soon."

"I'm thinking I should keep poking around down here," Fletcher said, "see if I can't get to know a few more of the locals."

"See if you hear anything about a thug named Gene. He was one of those I met tonight. Tall and skinny with stringy hair. Real sweet guy."

"Gene, huh?"

Fletcher turned up his glass.

"There can't be too many hideouts where they'd feel secure in keeping Jarvis for this long," he said. "It has to be somewhere that Romano's men come and go without fear of interference. Somebody knows where that is."

"I would imagine they've tightened ranks after tonight. They know people are on their trail. That makes your job even more dicey."

"I'll be all right. What are you going to do?"

"My mind seems to be going in circles. I was thinking about flying back to Knoxville early in the morning and meeting with the detective who was in charge of the investigation, maybe spelling out everything I know. I believe I can trust him. Now I'm thinking I might take a little side trip first. I want to keep pressing to get this nightmare over with. If I have to come back down here, I want to finish it."

"We're getting closer, no doubt. I'll let you know what I find out."

"I appreciate everything," Billy said. "Be careful."

The private investigator took one last sip, winked and walked out the door.

CHAPTER FIFTY-ONE

The Ravenel Bridge was a welcome sight in the distance. Spanning the Cooper River for over four miles, with its shiny white cables rising skyward like the sails of a tall ship, it was as much an architectural work of art as a busy highway connector between downtown Charleston and Mount Pleasant. For Billy, seeing the iconic bridge always meant Rachel was close by.

This time it all felt different as he made his way from Charleston International Airport.

Bradley King's house was a spectacular Mediterranean on Isle of Palms, just outside the Wild Dunes resort. It could have passed for a small hotel, and Billy had been an invited guest on many occasions. There was nothing better than taking a few days to relax, sample the fine cuisine of the low country and enjoy a little fun in the sun with Bradley and Elaine's sexy daughter.

For the next few days, the Kings would be down the coast at Hilton Head for a business conference. Bradley had emailed him to postpone their meeting, which was fine with Billy. It most likely was going to be an unpleasant experience with negative repercussions for his business and personal life alike. There was a good chance the developer had decided to cut ties.

Billy knew Rachel would be the only one home today and didn't bother to call ahead. He needed answers, plain and simple, and didn't want to give her time to prepare.

The concrete driveway circled a fountain that gushed water all around bronze herons feeding in an artistic marsh. Billy parked his rental car and admired the setting as he climbed the staircase and made his way to the door.

The doorbell echoed inside and he noticed movement through the sidelight of the grand entranceway. After a minute came the sound of a deadbolt lock releasing its hold. The big oak door opened and Rachel stood uncomfortably in front of him. Her face was without expression, her eyes lacking their usual sparkle. It was almost as if they were strangers.

"I told you not to come," she said. "Or I tried."

"I had to," Billy said. "We need to talk. Can I come in?"

Reluctantly, Rachel stepped aside to allow him to pass, closed the door and reset the lock. Without saying another word, she walked through the great hall and directly to a spacious deck in the back that offered a sweeping view of the Atlantic. Her gaze turned immediately to the rolling waves.

"How are you, Billy?" she said flatly.

"I think you know how I am. My brother just stabbed me in the back, my business is going to hell, I've got people who suddenly want to kill me. And, oh yeah, my girlfriend just packed up and left. I don't know why any of that is going on. So how are *you*?"

Rachel's eyes stayed fixed on the ocean. "What did you find out in New Orleans?" she said. "Do you know where Jarvis is?"

"No, but I'm beginning to understand what happened to him."

Billy studied her reaction. Blank.

"Romano's men grabbed him from right below where we were sleeping. John couldn't have stopped them, but he didn't want to, did he?"

No answer.

"There seems to be plenty of deceit going around," Billy said. "Why didn't you tell me you were involved in this?"

"What do you mean?"

"You were with John when he picked up the cocaine in Florida. The good-looking girl in the silver car. Right?"

Rachel turned and walked away.

"I didn't know what was going on," she said. "He just wanted to stop at this little bar and I waited in the car. We weren't there ten minutes."

"So you didn't end up with any of it? John didn't offer you any?"

"He offered, but I didn't want any. I'm not into that."

Billy began to grow angry.

"I don't believe you," he said. "I just hadn't noticed the signs. They were there all along."

He marched back into the house and up the staircase with her trailing in his wake. First, he went to Rachel's bedroom and began rifling through the nightstand drawers.

"Where is it?"

"Where's what?"

He pushed past her and into the bathroom and yanked open the medicine cabinet. Nothing there either.

Rachel's purse was hanging on the bedpost, and Billy grabbed it and turned it upside down as she lunged at him from behind. The contents spilled onto her sheets. Bingo: a brown glass vial more than half full of powder.

He held it between his fingers just inches from her face. "So you're not into *this*?" he said.

She slumped onto the bed and began to cry, but he was unmoved.

"What else have you been lying to me about?" Billy yelled. "Have you been sleeping with John, too?"

"No, it's not like that."

"You wouldn't have run unless something heavy was going on. You wouldn't have been scared away by me finding out you were doing cocaine with my brother. I mean, you're the big party girl anyway, right? What else is there? Do you know something about Jarvis, too?"

"Billy, you need to leave now. My parents would go off if they knew you were here. This whole thing has just freaked them out, and it's still freaking me out. Why did you even come?"

His stare burned into her like a laser.

"I just had to look into your eyes and see for myself. I know there's more you're not telling me. So it's going to end like this? You owe me an explanation at the very least."

"I just got in too deep. I wasn't ready for that kind of relationship, and I don't think you were either. We weren't really in love."

"But I trusted you," he said. "Like I trusted my brother. You both made a fool of me."

"Nobody set out to hurt you. Things just happened. It was good while it lasted ... for both of us. I don't know what else to say."

"Tell me about Paul Romano. Or Blaine Eldridge. They're both Charleston guys. Are they friends of yours?"

"I don't know who you're talking about," Rachel said. "You're getting paranoid."

"You're the one who ran off without any explanation. Of course, the picture is starting to clear."

Rachel grabbed his arm and looked him squarely in the face. "Please, Billy," she said. "Leave."

CHAPTER FIFTY-TWO

She could feel the whole house shake as Billy slammed the big door and strode angrily to his car. Moments later he was back on the road to Charleston.

Rachel stood at the window and finally was able to breathe a sigh of relief. That was a close call.

"You can come out now," she said.

A closet door opened and Paul Romano stepped into the foyer. He was smiling like the proverbial fox in the henhouse.

"That was intense," he said. "Your friend is about to snap. I thought I was going to have to rescue you."

"If you didn't hear, he knows about you," Rachel said. "He's putting everything together. The only thing he hasn't figured out is where Jarvis is. And you don't know?"

The smile left Paul's face. "I told you, I had nothing to do with kidnapping the football player. That was my father's doing."

"Then why did you call me late that night? You knew John and Jarvis were alone down at the dock. Your father knew, too. He told me when he called me on the way down here. How did he find out?"

Silence.

"So tell me what happened to Jarvis," she demanded.

"That's nothing for you to worry about."

Paul walked over to Rachel and pulled her close. She resisted at first but not for long.

"I thought you were finished with your father," she said, running her fingers through Paul's long hair. "That's why you came here to begin with. What happened to making a fresh start? You're a talented musician."

"I'm glad you noticed. Unfortunately, it doesn't pay the bills."

"It would be a waste to get involved with all the criminal stuff your father is into. Why go back to that? You'll all end up dead or in prison."

"My father convinced me that family means more," Paul said, "and it's hard to turn my back on him. I have to go home. If something happens to him, I'm next in line."

"Next in line? So that's it? You want to be the boss? A mafia boss? That's stupid."

"That's the way it happened for my father. He paid his dues and was rewarded when the time came. He's now a very rich man."

Rachel turned and walked away.

"I just wanted to stop and see you before I left," Paul said.

"Well, you've seen me, so go on. You're only going to cause trouble here anyway. You're already causing trouble."

"I thought you liked trouble."

"I don't like flirting with disaster. And that's what this will be once Billy finds out."

"It's not a good idea for him to be chasing around New Orleans," Paul said. "I guarantee you that won't end well for him."

Rachel walked back out to the deck with Paul trailing her.

"He's a very persistent guy, and this has made him crazy," she said. "He won't stop until he finds Jarvis; they're very close. He's going to find him, one way or another, and I'm afraid we're both going to get swept up in it."

"Why would you get swept up in it? You haven't done anything wrong."

"I talked to you that night, and that's enough. Billy isn't even aware that we know each other. That alone would be a huge problem."

"It's just a strange coincidence, all of this," Paul said.

He was not convincing. "I think it's more than that," she said. "You sought me out here once you found out who I was, and you didn't tell me who you really were. You've been using me for your own selfish purposes."

"Not true. It's been fun for both of us, you have to admit."

Paul walked to the refrigerator and casually pulled out a Palmetto pale ale.

"One for the road," he said. "I've got to make a few stops to round up my things before I head back. It's been an interesting time in Charleston. When will I see you again?"

"You won't," Rachel said. "This isn't going to work, me here and you in New Orleans. And I want no part of that down there. We're a long way apart in so many ways."

"And then in others, we're very close," Paul said, placing his hands gently around her waist. "We like to live dangerously. I want you to come to New Orleans."

CHAPTER FIFTY-THREE

Billy needed time to clear his head, time to be alone, so he just kept driving. Back across the bridge, past the airport and right on up Interstate 26 toward Tennessee. The Smoky Mountains were five hours away.

He hadn't slept much in weeks, and trying to put this jigsaw puzzle together had left him near the breaking point. The thoughts tumbled over and over in his mind.

If John was willing to undermine him, then Rachel had to be tainted, too. And if she knew Frank Romano was actively pursuing Jarvis Thompson, she had to know everyone around Billy was in danger and stayed quiet. But why?

He stared out at the Southern oaks, with Spanish moss draped elegantly from their branches. They became a blur. The battle with fatigue was becoming greater, and he turned on the air conditioning and put his face to the vent. *Keep pushing*, he thought.

About a hundred miles into the drive, as he neared Columbia, there was a ring from his phone in the console. It was Trey Birchfield.

"Tell me something good," Billy said.

The response wasn't what he wanted to hear. "I wish I could."

The reporter went on to say that the Knoxville police were scaling back the active search for Jarvis Thompson locally. They had exhausted all leads and were now going on the theory that the football star had been taken against his will and transported out of the area. They couldn't be sure he was still alive but were working with the FBI and other law enforcement agencies. They still had no motive.

"From what I'm hearing, your brother has confessed to his part in this," Birchfield said. "He admitted that the cocaine belonged to him. All of it."

"What about the thugs who almost killed him?" Billy said.

"He said he didn't know who they were but thought they were mafia types. Maybe from New Orleans. That just confirmed what the detectives were thinking. They aren't real happy that his story didn't come out earlier."

"Is John in jail?"

"No, he bonded out," Birchfield said. "I think your father came and took him home. From what I hear, he was a real mess."

Billy was more worried about his father, the toll all of this was taking on him, and he picked up the pace on the interstate. The North Carolina border wasn't far away.

"I appreciate you letting me know, Trey. Where does this leave things as far as the *Journal's* reporting? It's important to keep people focused on the investigation."

"I'll stay on the story, of course. Everybody here is going to be hugely interested until Jarvis turns up, one way or another. But we're not the *New York Times* and, big as this story is in Knoxville, I don't know how many resources the newspaper will devote to it if there's not much new to report. It looks like the focus of the investigation is shifting. We'll see where it goes."

Billy thought about that for a few seconds.

"I have some new information that I think you would be very interested in," he said. "You could end up with the exclusive on this whole deal."

"Tell me more."

"I will when I get back to town. It may be tomorrow."

"All right," Birchfield said. "You call me at any time of day, it doesn't matter. I can imagine what you have to be going through, and I want to help you on this."

Billy didn't have many allies left, and Birchfield might prove to be one of the most valuable in cracking the case. He had the public forum and the contacts. He could get information.

As he sped toward Tennessee, Billy tried to imagine where Jarvis was and what he was feeling. Days had turned into weeks. *Was the kid still holding out hope?*

Billy held the phone to his face and thought about calling his father to see what had transpired with John. But he wasn't ready for that conversation just yet.

Another ring broke his rambling train of thought. Mark Fletcher.

"Talk to me," Billy said.

"I've met some interesting people this morning," Fletcher said. "A couple of these guys used to do some dirty work for Romano, and they had a falling out over money or something. They're fortunate to still be alive to tell about it."

"Have they heard anything about Jarvis?"

"Nothing they were willing to share with me, but there's something else. I think I may know who your friend Gene is."

"Really?"

"His name is Eugene Casey. He's an ex-soldier who did a couple of tours of duty in Afghanistan. They said he was a notorious sniper, killed a lot of bad guys. He apparently snapped one day during a firefight in some village over there and they had to shut him down. The army discharged him and sent him home."

"To New Orleans?"

"Yep," Fletcher said. "He's supposed to be one of Romano's most trusted men now; they grew up together. Doesn't say much and has a crazy look in his eyes, like he's still waiting for insurgents to show up at any minute. These guys I talked to said he's a very scary dude, even by their standards."

"That's him," Billy said. "What about his partner?"

"Not sure yet. I ran out of time and will try to get back in touch with them later today. These are the nervous types, armed to the teeth, always moving around and looking over their shoulders. I've dealt with hundreds like them. They're in a bad way right now and are fishing for a little cash. Seems like a good tradeoff for some information."

"I agree. Do you need me to wire some money?"

"No, I can handle it, but your tab is rising quickly," Fletcher said. "I'm going to meet them down in the French Quarter. I'll let you know when I find out more."

"Don't put yourself on the line," Billy said. "There's nobody there to back you up."

"I'll be fine," Fletcher said. "I know what I'm doing."

The news gave Billy a little jolt of energy. *One step closer*, he thought. On to the Smokies.

CHAPTER FIFTY-FOUR

Billy was mentally prepared for another confrontation with his brother by the time he reached his old stomping grounds in Sevierville.

He had been so tied up with his business over the last year, he couldn't remember the last time he was home. He knew his father enjoyed the company, but it felt like some sort of barrier had grown between them. The situation with John made tensions much worse. It was better if Billy kept his distance.

Now he couldn't stay away.

The brick ranch came into view, and he eased to a stop in front and looked around. The neighborhood always had a nostalgic feel. The spacious yard was once the hub of the block, with kids flowing in and out for all sorts of activities. There was a daily baseball game in the summer and knock-down-drag-out football scraps in the fall.

Where did the years go?

A row of white pines that were once knee-high saplings had taken over the outfield, and a small pond occupied the space where home plate used to be. His mother had always wanted a pond.

Franklin Beckett's red pickup was the only vehicle in the driveway, and Billy parked beside it.

It took a minute to muster the courage to go inside, but he exhaled a deep breath and walked through the carport and into the kitchen. His father was reading the newspaper at the table.

"I heard what happened," Billy said. "Where is John?"

Franklin offered an uneasy shrug. "He came back here with me this morning and got some stuff together and left. I don't know where he was going."

"Have you tried calling him?"

"He never picks up anymore. I'm really worried about him. This whole thing with your football star has torn him apart."

"It's torn everybody apart," Billy said. "I tried to help John, and you see what I got. He stabbed me in the back."

"Your brother loves you, Billy. His head just isn't right. Hasn't been for a while."

"You'll have to forgive me, but I don't feel real loved right now. And I'm not sure my head is quite right either. I'm thinking some bad thoughts."

"I told you about tying yourself to these high-risk athletes," his father said. "It's hard to live a normal life when you have to depend on them. One day everything is great, and the next day it's all to hell. They can't be trusted any more than the billionaires that own them."

Billy couldn't absorb much more. His eyes were about to close.

"I give up, Dad. Would you mind if I laid down for a while in the back bedroom? If I don't get some sleep, I'm going to keel over."

"Go ahead. Maybe your brother will be here when you get up."

"Wake me up if he comes."

Billy walked down the hall to his old room and didn't even bother to take off his clothes. He was out as soon as his head hit the pillow.

***

It was almost midnight when he opened his eyes again. A quick nap had turned into six hours, and it would have been longer if not for the nagging thought that finally stirred him awake.

What about Mark Fletcher?

The private investigator should have met again with Romano's former henchmen hours ago. He probably knew who Gene's partner was by now, and maybe a whole lot more.

Billy checked his phone for new messages, but there were none. He got up and staggered down the hallway and into the living room. All was quiet, except for the tick-tock of the old grandfather clock in the corner that had been there for as long as he could remember. His father had already gone to bed, and there were no signs John had been back.

He sat on the couch and began to slip on his shoes while he fumbled with his phone. No answer in New Orleans; Fletcher's voice mail picked up.

"Just touching base," Billy said. "It's getting late and I'm heading home from my father's. You call me and let me know what you heard, no matter what time it is. I won't be able to sleep anyway thinking about it."

There would be no call tonight, and no sign of his brother.

PART III

CHAPTER FIFTY-FIVE

John Beckett stood on the rubber and took in the surroundings. After all these years, the mound still looked and felt the same.

The wind was biting and blowing in, the pitcher's friend. He stared toward home plate, envisioning another poor batter who was in way over his head. How many strikes, how many unhittable pitches, had he thrown from this very spot?

The cheers of family and friends still echoed in his head.

John was a can't-miss prospect, and everyone in town knew it. Especially Billy. No one enjoyed watching a baseball fired from that cannon of an arm more than John's older brother. There was a sense of pride built from all those summer days when Billy would don the catcher's gear and squat in the hot sun, analyzing every delivery. He reveled in John's successes, one after another, and dreamed right along with him.

Franklin Beckett used to take his boys down to Atlanta to catch a couple of Braves games every summer, and they all decided then that John would look best wearing the red, white and blue. The picture never changed in any of their minds; John would indeed be a Brave, the young gun in the starting rotation with the Hall of Famers – Smoltz, Glavine and Maddux.

Years later, when he was working in the city, it was hard for Billy to go out to Turner Field without imagining what might have been. His dad would drive down and join him occasionally, but John never went back. It was too painful.

Near the end at Florida State, after John had lost his velocity and was being roughed up by light-hitting infielders, the once invincible left-hander no longer felt like the tallest man on the diamond. The pitcher's mound was a scary place, and there was nowhere to hide.

John pulled a half-pint of bourbon from his jacket and knelt in the red dirt, scanning the empty parking lot and grandstands at Sevier County High School. He took a big drink and wiped his eyes. There were no games today, only memories and regrets.

"I'm sorry, Billy," he said. "For everything."

Billy had been standing in his kitchen, still waiting to hear from Mark Fletcher when his brother's name appeared on the caller ID. For some reason, the anger that had been penned up inside him gave way to concern before the conversation even started.

"John, where are you?" he said.

"I'm lost ... just lost. And I don't want to find my way back."

"What are you talking about?"

"I've done some bad things, Billy. Our mother would be so ashamed. She always believed in me, right to the end. She was a fool."

His tone was ominous, alarming. "I don't like the sound of this, John," Billy said. "Tell me where you are. Let me come help."

"You can't help me this time, big brother."

Billy was suddenly afraid. He tried to buy time, pull out some pleasant memories. Anything to keep his brother talking.

"Don't you remember all those all-star games where we were in tight spots? You were the strong one, the one everybody depended on. You were the guy who picked up the team and carried us. You still have that in you."

"That was a long time ago," John said. "I'm weak now."

"No, you're not. You have an addiction, and you can beat it. I'll help you."

There was no answer.

John took another gulp and began to sob quietly.

"You know I couldn't have made it this far without you, Billy. And how did I pay you back? Conspired with your enemies to set up your star client. I put everybody here in danger. And Rachel ... that never should have happened."

"Rachel?"

John turned up the bottle and finished with one mighty swallow.

He could hear the cheers growing.

Louder. Louder. Louder.

There was a small revolver in his left hand now.

John raised it to his temple, calm and steady.

"I love you, Billy," he said. "Tell Dad I love him, too. Please forgive me."

CHAPTER FIFTY-SIX

It didn't take long to find the body. A custodian at the high school had heard the shot, and police were on the gruesome scene within minutes. The gun and empty liquor bottle laid by John's side.

Another life once filled with such promise had come to a tragic end, and word traveled fast in Sevierville.

By late afternoon the high school field had become a memorial. Flowers and baseballs with scribbled notes of condolence were piling up on all sides of the mound.

The suicide rattled the town, which is a gateway to a bustling national park and tourist mecca but close-knit all the same. Everyone knew and respected the Becketts.

Franklin had been on the police force for three decades, and his wife was active in virtually every civic organization around. The boys were local celebrities in their own right. Billy, in fact, had quarterbacked Sevier County to the only state championship in its football history. The fans had never forgotten.

John was a sophomore receiver on that team, a big target with great hands, but the spring and summer months were when he did his best work. He'd stride out of the dugout, slowly but with supreme confidence, and take the mound with the bill of his cap pulled low. He knew all eyes were upon him, and he loved it. John always wanted to be the center of attention.

And so he was again in this twisted way, gone at thirty-three, and his father and brother were left to try to make sense of it.

The psychological wounds of Anna Beckett's death were suddenly fresh again for Billy. The guilt was overwhelming, but he tried to bottle it up. At the moment, he felt more numb than anything else.

"Is there anything I can get you?" Billy said to his father. Grief-stricken, Franklin stared blankly out the window. He had experienced heartache on many levels, but this was the cruelest blow of all. A man isn't supposed to bury his son.

Billy sat on the couch and rubbed his face, trying to stimulate the blood flow to his brain. He couldn't afford to be exhausted; he had to be strong.

He needed to call Sam Jamison, an old family friend, to make funeral arrangements. There were relatives to contact and plenty of other details to attend to, sad details he never could have imagined.

Billy knew he was losing control. The good life he had constructed was coming undone, piece by piece. A burning rage was starting to build inside of him.

"I don't know how things have gone so wrong so quickly," he said, "but I can't sit back and take it anymore. I'm going to get these animals, if it's the last thing I do. I promise you that."

Franklin said nothing.

Billy wasn't sure where he was going, but he grabbed his coat and headed toward the front door. His father could have tried to stop him. He didn't.

Before Billy could turn the knob, the doorbell rang and he was standing eye to eye with Steve Thomas, a Sevierville detective. Neither knew what to say.

Thomas and Franklin Beckett went back a long way. They worked on dozens of investigations together through the years and had become the best of friends. Their boys played in the same sports leagues and the families used to barbeque on weekends, even took beach vacations together a couple of times.

And now Thomas was here to offer condolences, and maybe some clarity, in the aftermath of a gut-wrenching tragedy. The pain showed plainly on his face.

"I'm so sorry about John," he said, giving Billy a hug on the porch. "Can I speak to your father?"

Billy pointed him inside, and Franklin stood up and greeted him with a long embrace.

"I can't tell you how bad I'm hurting for you right now," Thomas said. He took a deep breath. "Did you have any idea that John was struggling to this extent?"

"I knew he hadn't been happy, but no," Franklin said. "He just felt like he'd let everybody down and there was no way to make things right again."

"So you had spoken to him earlier?"

"No, but he called Billy. He was at the ballpark."

"What did he say to you, Billy?" Thomas said.

"He just kept apologizing, and I tried to calm him down. I had a bad sense from the start. Then ..."

Billy closed his eyes and bowed his head. "He said to forgive him and then I heard the shot."

There was silence in the room.

"I don't want to get into a lot of this now," Thomas said, "but if you'll bear with me..."

"It's okay, Steve," Franklin said. "I understand."

"Let me ask you about the Jarvis Thompson case. I know John was involved to some extent in whatever went down at Billy's house that night."

"That's right. He had a drug habit that was worse than any of us realized. It drove him to make some very bad decisions. That's why we're standing here right now."

Thomas pulled a folded sheet of paper out of his jacket.

"The reason I ask is that one of our officers found this in John's pocket this morning. I'm assuming there's a connection here."

He handed the note to Franklin. The block letters had been written in red ink, the message short.

DON'T LET THEM WIN

Franklin rubbed his thumb across the paper and eased back into his chair. Billy's face was flushed with anger. Neither man spoke.

"I need to keep this as part of the investigation," Thomas said, "but I thought you would want to see it. As the lead investigator for our department, I'm confident that law enforcement officials will continue to work hard across the region to solve the Jarvis Thompson case. That's the way things should proceed."

He hesitated.

"As a friend, I understand your frustration. This has been going on far too long."

"Damn right," Billy said. "Reputations lost. And now lives – my own brother. How much longer?"

He grabbed his coat and left the house.

CHAPTER FIFTY-SEVEN

The last thing Billy was expecting was a call from Mark Fletcher's wife. The message was waiting on his phone when he climbed into the rental car.

"I'm sorry to bother you, but this is Anita Fletcher. I'm at home in Atlanta and was just a little concerned about Mark. He was supposed to call me last night; we had a couple of important financial matters we needed to wrap up. That's why he had to come home from Florida earlier. I never heard from him and just wondered if you had. I would appreciate it if you could give me a call."

Billy started replaying their last conversation, which had gotten lost in his mind. Fletcher said he might be out of touch for a few days but should have reported back to him by now. And he sure should have called his wife.

The PI's phone kicked to voice mail immediately. Billy's anxiety level continued to rise as he dialed Anita Fletcher back.

"Anita, I'm sorry I missed your call," he said. "I have a problem at home here and haven't spoken to Mark. Is something wrong?"

"I don't know what he's working on for you, Billy, but it isn't like Mark not to call when he knows I have something to take care of here. I'm afraid to do anything until I talk to him."

Billy tried to put his misery aside for a brief moment. Fletcher forgetting to call, both him and his wife? It wasn't likely. Unable to call? Perhaps.

Billy still wanted to be reassuring.

"I'm sure he's all right," he said. "You know those Texans; sometimes they get their minds locked onto something and can't let go. I haven't been able to try Mark today, but I will. Maybe he'll call you in the meanwhile."

"Thank you, Billy. I don't mean to interfere. I just want to be sure everything is all right."

All right? Nothing was all right. Billy started the car and headed toward Knoxville. His head was swimming.

He needed to give his brother a proper burial.

He needed to know Mark Fletcher was safe.

He needed to find Jarvis Thompson.

He needed to save his business.

At this point, he was desperate enough to throw a Hail Mary, so he called Trey Birchfield.

"I didn't know if I'd hear from you again," the reporter said. "Really sorry about your brother. That's not something I expected to be writing about today."

"Listen, Trey, I need to turn in a rental car at the airport," Billy said. "How would you like to pick me up there, outside Hertz? That'll give us some time to talk."

"I can be there in an hour."

***

Birchfield arrived right on time, and Billy folded himself into the passenger seat of the small convertible without really knowing what direction their discussion would take.

"Thanks for the lift," he said.

Birchfield studied him carefully. "It's okay; I don't really know what to say. I'm surprised you're out here and not with your father right now. And I'm really surprised you're calling reporters for rides."

"I guess the circle has gotten smaller. Must be a bad sign, huh? No shortage of bad signs right now."

Birchfield merged into traffic and turned down the radio.

"So tell me, how can we help each other on this?" he said. "Wasn't that the idea?"

Billy sat quietly for a few seconds. He was working on the fly, something he used to be very good at.

"I'm driving to New Orleans in a couple of days. How would you like to ride with me?" he said. "I think a lot of news could come out of the trip, and you'd have a front-row seat."

"A front-row seat to *what* exactly?"

"I can't promise you anything, but I have a feeling the whole Jarvis Thompson saga will reveal itself. Isn't that what reporters live for – an exclusive story the whole country is interested in?"

A crooked smile crossed Birchfield's lips. "Why are you offering me this?"

"Because I think I can trust you," Billy said. "And because your skills may come in handy down there. We'll have to gather some information to put things together, and everyone says you're very good at that. Here's the rub, though: I don't want anybody else to know you're with me. That includes your bosses, and your wife."

"So I'm supposed to take who knows how long off work without telling anybody where I'm going and what I'm doing. Even my wife."

"Right," Billy said. "If that doesn't work for you, forget it. I'll go by myself and you can read about how it all turned out in some other newspaper."

"Give me a minute to process this," Birchfield said as he drove along in interstate traffic. Finally, he looked over at Billy and nodded.

"Okay. I'll tell my boss I need to burn a few vacation days to unwind; I'm due for a vacation anyway. I'll tell my wife I'm going on a business trip. This better be one hell of a story."

"No guts, no glory. Isn't that what they say?" Billy said. "You just have to keep it under wraps until the right time. No one else will know."

"Let's do it then. By the way, where am I taking you?"

"To my house, Rocky Top Estates, out by the river. I have a lot of planning to do." Tears began to pool again in Billy's eyes. "I have to say goodbye to my brother."

CHAPTER FIFTY-EIGHT

The townspeople braved a rainy afternoon to pay their last respects to John Beckett, a man they only thought they knew.

A steady stream of mourners filed through the stately corridors of Jamison Funeral Home, which was used to handling services for Sevierville's most prominent families. There had been an overflow crowd just a couple of days earlier when one of Dolly Parton's cousins was laid to rest.

The collection of John's pictures was scattered about for the people to look at as they slowly made their way to the front of the chapel. Snapshots in time.

John at Florida State, at the height of his powers, locked on his target as he delivered a pitch with all his might.

He and Billy hoisting an AAU championship trophy in front of their proud parents, big smiles all around.

Sitting on the hood of a police cruiser as a boy at his father's station.

With his mother at Myrtle Beach, arm in arm, not long before her death.

The adoring way Anna Beckett looked at her youngest son said everything about the bond between them. If there was any comfort in this tragedy, it was that maybe they were together again.

Franklin and Billy were greeting the masses in the chapel, beside a closed oak casket, and from the look of things they were going to be there for a while. The funeral would follow, and a graveside service would be held across the street at Roselawn Gardens.

It took more than three hours for the line to clear. By then the chapel pews were almost full. The preacher walked out and started to escort Billy and his father to a side viewing area.

Fighting to stay composed, Billy took just a moment to scan the congregation. The faces were mostly a blur, but there along the aisle on the back row, a solitary figure caught his attention.

Rachel.

The sight of her sitting there in a black dress, dabbing at her eyes with a tissue, stopped Billy in his tracks. It took a lot of nerve for her to show up.

Franklin tugged at Billy's arm and guided him to a seat around the corner with perhaps fifteen other relatives, distant aunts and uncles and cousins. He couldn't have named half of them.

The preacher was a stranger, too – a newcomer at the Methodist church where the Becketts were lifelong members – but he spoke eloquently about forgiveness and redemption, topics that certainly applied in this case. He then recited Psalm 23, maybe the only piece of scripture John knew. *The Lord is my shepherd ...*

One of John's old schoolmates sang Amazing Grace at the end, and there was a prayer and everyone was invited to attend the burial service. It was short and fairly uplifting under the circumstances, the way John would have wanted it.

Billy walked quickly around the corner to check the crowd as it began to disperse, but she was gone. He turned to his father.

"Did you see her?"

"Who?" Franklin said. He was in another place entirely.

CHAPTER FIFTY-NINE

The finality began to sink in the moment they turned and staggered away from the casket. It was just the two of them now.

Billy felt completely numb as he walked through the wet grass, shoulder to shoulder with his father, toward the black hearse at the bottom of the hill. Dozens of friends and acquaintances stood under umbrellas and watched them pass. Another surreal scene at Roselawn Gardens.

A funeral home attendant opened a limousine door and Franklin stepped in. Billy was about to join him when he heard that familiar voice call his name. Rachel was alone on the other side of the street, rain dripping from her hair and down that beautiful face.

"Wait just a minute, Dad," Billy said. He closed the door and stood still by the limo for a moment.

They were locked in each other's gaze as Billy walked over to her. "Why did you come?" he said softly.

"I needed to be here. John was a good man ... he didn't deserve this. No one does. I'm sorry."

"And that's it?"

She hesitated and dropped her head.

"I've been thinking a lot about us, too. I do owe you an explanation."

Billy walked back to the limo, leaned in and said a few words. The driver handed him a small umbrella and then left with his father.

Rachel had turned and was starting slowly toward her car. Billy opened the umbrella and they walked close together.

"You were right. I did know about the cocaine," she said. "It seemed innocent at the time. We were on the road, and getting high helped pass the time. John was fun to party with; it was never more than that."

"Did you know where the stuff came from?"

"Not at first, but John told me later. It was Jarvis's father who brought it to him down in Florida. The whole thing had been set up."

"Charles?" Billy said. "How did he get involved in this?"

"I don't know, but he was the guy who handed off the package. He was supposed to be trying to get Jarvis to turn against you, with John's help. It wasn't apparent to me that he was just working for Romano."

Billy's eyes narrowed in that familiar way.

"And what about Romano's son? How does he figure into this?"

"I don't know, honestly," Rachel said. "He's a musician and I got to know him after he moved to Charleston and was playing around town with his band. We're just friends."

"When was the last time you saw him?"

"He was playing in Charleston several weeks ago."

"Didn't you know his last name and ever put the pieces together?" Billy said.

"He didn't use Romano. He was Paul Richards to me – Paul Richards and the Hit Men."

"Sounds like a hell of a coincidence that all these people have closed in on me. Unbelievable, really. And you have no idea where Jarvis is?"

"I don't; you have to believe me," Rachel said. "I asked Paul and he said he didn't know either."

"So you've talked to Paul recently?"

"Just briefly on the phone. He was collecting his stuff to go home. He should be back in New Orleans now."

Rachel unlocked her Mercedes as they walked up. They got in and everything was quiet for a minute. Billy was trying hard to clear his mind and process this new information.

"So when did you know Frank Romano was behind this?" he said.

"He called me on my phone when I was driving back to Charleston, just to make sure I got the message. He was blackmailing me to leave Knoxville for good, to leave you."

Rachel shook her head. "That was a terrible day."

"There have been a lot of those lately," Billy said. "But things are about to change."

"What are you going to do?"

"I'm going to New Orleans to find Jarvis. This nightmare is going to end, one way or another."

"I don't like the sound of that."

Rachel said she was afraid of how things would turn out and was planning to go back to Charleston to lay low for a while. Maybe she'd get into the family business and start fresh. Billy knew she wasn't going to be pulled back into this odyssey with Jarvis.

"I probably won't come back this way again," she said. "I just wanted to be here today. For John, and for you. Our time together really meant a lot to me ... I'm so sorry for the way it ended. You deserved better, and so did John. I hope you don't hate me."

Billy left it right there. He got out of the car, patted the top and looked to the heavens, which were raining down upon him as she drove away.

CHAPTER SIXTY

After two weeks in captivity, the Autumn Blaze no longer resembled the elite football player that had grabbed the nation's attention.

Wearing an orange jumpsuit, like the Orleans Parish inmates, he had lost several pounds. Gone, too, was that unmistakable air of confidence. Escape was no longer an option. Jarvis wasn't sure he could run, even if he had the chance.

The heavy door opened and daylight filtered into the small, dank room. He sat up on the dirty mattress on the floor and found himself in the shadow of a large man standing over him.

"So I finally meet the great Jarvis Thompson," came a booming voice. "You don't look so great, kid."

Jarvis squinted, trying to adjust his vision, and said nothing. One of his ankles was shackled to the wall. Like a prisoner of war, he could see no clear future, no way out. But what kind of war was this?

Frank Romano pulled up a chair and parked his oversized frame, guarded by two armed men at the door. Their silhouettes resembled Tommy and Gene, but Jarvis couldn't be sure. Several different men had been around since he was first brought to the old warehouse and locked in a storage room in the back. Even in his condition, it took three to wrestle him through the door and subdue him.

"We still have those nasty syringes if we need them," Romano said. "We're not going to have to go through that again, are we? You have to stay calm, for your own good."

Jarvis still said nothing.

The crime boss turned and one of the guards handed him something wrapped in thin white paper. He flipped it to Jarvis, who instinctively made the grab. Food.

"It's a po' boy," Romano said. "Welcome to New Orleans."

Jarvis hesitated and then peeled back the paper and stuffed one end of the sandwich in his mouth. Romano looked at him curiously. He enjoyed having Billy Beckett's famous protégé under his control, being so close to the agent's heart and soul. There was even a touch of awe. So *this* was a world-class athlete.

"I hear your football team is really missing you," Romano said. "Are you missing those guys?"

Jarvis remained silent, his face a blank slate.

"What about your agent? Bet you're missing him, too. You know he's why you're here."

Romano had finally struck a nerve.

Jarvis took a sip of water and wiped his mouth. "Why do you say that?" he said.

"He's a lowlife, and so you're soiled, too."

"Because he's a sports agent? I thought you liked those guys. I kept hearing about how you wanted me to sign with Sonny Bradley. Isn't he your boy?"

"Not anymore," Romano said. "I don't care who you sign with, as long as it's not Billy Beckett. And that's assuming you ever have a pro football career, which is a pretty big assumption at this point."

Jarvis took another big bite of the sandwich. He was starting to perk up.

"So what did Billy ever do to you?" he said.

"Let's just say I have an old score to settle with him. I'm a vengeful man, I admit it."

"Does that mean you're just going to kill both of us? Your men could have done that at Billy's house that night."

"That would have been too easy," Romano said. "I don't want to kill Billy Beckett right now. I want to control him. I want him to suffer. Losing you, losing his brother, losing his pretty girlfriend, losing his business ... maybe after he's suffered long enough, I'll have one of the boys put a bullet in his head. Gene could have already done it more than once."

"What about me?"

"We'll see what your life is worth. You're a football star, but I don't really give a damn about athletes. They're spoiled and greedy, and in the grand scheme of things there's no real money in managing their affairs. Just prestige, and I already have that."

Jarvis was now more perplexed than afraid. His life in the projects had taught him a few things about violent men. They were insecure, and you could get in their heads if you did it right. You just had to tread carefully.

"What prestige?" he said. "All I see is a fat guy who runs a drug ring and ruins lives."

Romano chuckled.

"Are you trying to make me mad, kid? That takes balls, especially when you're sitting there chained to the wall. You obviously have a lot bigger balls than your old man did."

"So you know him, too?"

"Knew him. Very briefly. He was a loser, and I'm sure he was a pathetic excuse for a father. But he might still be around if he just knew how to follow instructions. Of course, he'd be out there somewhere killing himself slowly with all the drugs and booze. We just sped up the process."

Jarvis sat back against the wall and ate the last of the sandwich. "What do you mean?"

"I mean Charles, your father, is long gone. He couldn't dig his way out of that old Domino sugarcane field in Chalmette. You better hope he's the last in your family to suffer an untimely death. You people are living dangerously."

The big man stood and turned to leave.

"How long are you going to keep me here?" Jarvis said.

"I haven't decided, but you can't stay forever. Too many people are looking for you; I know Billy Beckett is. He's got a lot invested in you becoming a big NFL star."

"I'll sign with another agent if you'll just let me go and leave Billy alone."

Romano laughed.

"I've got another idea. Let's see if we can't lure Billy down here and have a little chat. We'll make it easy for him. If he was going to the cops, I'm sure he would have

SCOTT PRATT

already done it. I know he'd love to end up being your hero. Wouldn't it be something if we had both of you guys right here, together again? I can see it now."

The crime boss lit a cigarette and narrowed his eyes, like he was envisioning the scene, finally having Billy Beckett under his thumb. There was a trace of euphoria on his face.

"It's been a real pleasure meeting you, kid," he said. "This is probably not going to end well, but you never know. It's kind of like a Hail Mary pass. Sometimes you get lucky."

The door closed and Jarvis was again alone in the darkness.

CHAPTER SIXTY-ONE

The first order of business was to find Mark Fletcher. The private eye had been out of touch for days, and the alarm was growing as Billy and Trey Birchfield rolled into the Big Easy late on an overcast afternoon.

Birchfield knew the story by now and was chomping at the bit to get to the bottom of it. He had been talking to his reporter friend at the *New Orleans Tribune* on the way down and wanted to see what may have transpired in the last few hours.

Billy dropped him at the door of the newspaper and headed to a hotel down in the Warehouse District. Birchfield was cleared through security and took the elevator to the third floor. His friend, David Mettetal, was standing there to greet him when the door opened.

"It's about time you made it down here," Mettetal said. Birchfield stepped into the hallway and shook his hand. "Too bad it's not Mardi Gras season. The town will only be crazy instead of insane. Come on in."

Mettetal was a veteran of the police beat and about as connected as any journalist in the city. If the cops knew something, it wasn't long before he knew, too.

The men walked through the newsroom and sat down at his crowded cubicle in the corner. They had been classmates at Fordham University, and both left journalism school with designs on making a difference. Judging from all the plaques on the wall, Birchfield could see his friend had done well.

"Coffee?" Mettetal said.

"No, thanks. Maybe we can have a beverage later."

"How long are you in town?"

"That's a good question. As long as it takes, I guess. My boss thinks I'm on vacation."

Birchfield was anxious to learn if there had been any scuttlebutt about Fletcher's whereabouts since they had spoken earlier.

"So this PI has been down here looking into the Jarvis Thompson case," Mettetal said, "and now nobody knows where he is?"

"That's about it. Like I told you, he was supposed to be meeting again with these two guys that used to work for Romano. The calls quit coming a few days ago. We're afraid maybe he got too close."

"Well, he hasn't turned up yet, and that's probably a good thing. When it comes to Romano, missing persons usually aren't missing for long. They're found floating in a pond, or laying in a ditch along the road somewhere. It's never a very subtle message."

"Like Sonny Bradley?"

"Exactly," Mettetal said. "And just like that case, there never seems to be enough evidence to tie Romano to it. He's always just out of reach. That's why I suppose he'd be bold enough to kidnap someone like Jarvis Thompson, although it's still crazy to think about."

"So the cops know what's going on but haven't been able to stop him?"

"We have some hard-core criminals down here – it's still one of the most dangerous cities in the country – and Romano is getting more notorious all the time. There's a certain glamor to it, I guess, and his organization is so tight-knit, the cops are never able to pin these murders on him. There have probably been a couple dozen like that this year, still sitting in the unsolved file. Of course, the way some of the cops operate, you can't be sure what's going on behind the scenes."

"What do you mean?"

"I mean corruption is rampant," Mettetal said. "You can't trust a lot of the boys in blue, or the politicians. Some of them have been flat-out bought by Romano, and he's getting his money's worth."

Birchfield glanced at his watch. He needed to get moving.

"So what about Jarvis Thompson?" he said. "The Knoxville police have basically given up on finding him up there. It sounded like the investigation was coming your way."

"I've heard that, and everybody I've talked to is baffled by it. One of the best college football players in the country snatched from his agent's home like that, without a trace. Just vanishes, no ransom notes or anything. That's definitely a new one."

"Let me ask you this," Birchfield said. "If Jarvis were being held down here, any idea where Romano might hide him?"

"It's hard to say, because that gang has so many places where all sorts of crimes are happening. A lot of Romano's activities have been traced to the Crescent Park area in the past. Development is supposed to be picking up out there – it's a great view of the city – but there are still a lot of old industrial sites and warehouses that haven't been in operation for a while. You could hide just about anything, or anybody, in that area. There are some other possibilities down along the canal, too."

"I'll be in town until we figure something out, so let's keep in touch. I don't want to take any more of your time now. Maybe you can buy me that beer before I leave, like the old days."

Birchfield got up and was shaking his friend's hand when the phone on the desk rang. Mettetal picked up the receiver, and a solemn look came over his face. The call didn't last long.

"Maybe bad news," he said. "They just found a body in Housley Park. I have to go to work."

CHAPTER SIXTY-TWO

irchfield asked if he could tag along and soon found himself at the grisly murder scene out on the northeastern edge of town. Housley Park was another rough-and-tumble slice of public green space where much of the public would never dare to go.

The victim had been stabbed several times and already had a sheet draped over him on the ground when they arrived. The area was marked off by yellow police tape. Detective Jake Allary was talking with another cop while the coroner prepared for the body to be moved.

Allary saw the reporters approach and walked over to the tapeline. Mettetal greeted him with familiarity.

"What do we have, Jake?"

"White guy in his late fifties or so. Didn't have a wallet or any ID on him. No cell phone. Could have been a robbery victim, but considering the way he was carved up, I'd say there was some serious malice involved."

"Who found him?"

"A homeless lady noticed the body in the bushes behind that bench over there. She spends a lot of time roaming around in the park; our officers know her."

Mettetal surveyed the area with an experienced eye and jotted down a few notes on his pad. The smell of death lingered in the air.

"Sorry to spoil your dinner, David," the detective said. "And mine."

"Not the first time, or the last, I'm sure," Mettetal said. "Anything unusual about this gentleman?"

"Not really. Well-dressed, though, for a guy hanging around this area."

"Any chance he was killed elsewhere and dumped here?"

"Would have been a mess to move. Looks like it happened here, probably last night or early this morning. The hoodlums around here are savages. It's like they don't fear anybody anymore."

Mettetal waved Birchfield closer and introduced him to the detective. He explained that they were looking for Mark Fletcher.

"Trey, do you know what your missing private eye looks like?" Mettetal said.

"I don't, but Billy is on his way. If this is his friend ..." The thought just trailed off and the detective went back to work.

The body had been placed on a gurney and was being wheeled to the coroner's van for transport to the morgue as Billy pulled into the parking lot. He jumped out of his car and walked quickly to the gathering.

"Tell me this isn't Mark," he said.

"They don't know," Birchfield said, "but they were waiting for a possible ID."

Billy looked at the men with grave concern. His face was ashen. "Okay," he said.

Mettetal called over the detective, who raised the tape barrier and escorted Billy to the back of the van. The agent had once litigated all sorts of criminal activity but had never seen a dead man laid out before him like this, certainly not a friend. He prepared for the worst.

Allary reached over and pulled back the bloody sheet.

One look and Billy's knees almost buckled. He turned to vomit in the grass.

Mark Fletcher.

"I'm sorry," the detective said. "Why don't you guys take him over there and sit down for a minute."

The three sat silently on a bench for several minutes before Mettetal excused himself to gather more information about the murder. Finally, Billy was composed enough to speak.

"This is my fault," he said. "Mark wouldn't have been here if it wasn't for me. I put him in this position."

"You can't blame yourself," Birchfield said. "The guy was a veteran detective; he understood the danger. He wanted to help solve this."

"And now look where we are. He's dead and we still don't know where Jarvis is. We haven't solved anything."

"We're getting closer, though. You can feel it."

Billy leaned back and covered his face with his hands. After a long, deep breath, he said, "I have to call Anita."

He got up and was walking away as Allary approached Birchfield.

"Did you say his name is Billy Beckett?" he asked.

"That's right."

"It just occurred to me." The detective held up a business card with a distinctive orange logo: Billy Beckett Enterprises. "We found this in the man's back pocket. Haven't we seen this act before?"

CHAPTER SIXTY-THREE

For the second time in a week, Billy had to be the bearer of the worst possible news. A loved one had died a violent death, and he didn't know why.

Anita Fletcher handled the shock far better than he could have expected. Maybe she was simply numb. Or maybe being a detective's wife all those years, she had run through the awful scenarios many times before in her mind. The call had just never come, until now.

Speaking in measured tones, she wanted to know the facts: Did they have a suspect in custody? How had it happened? Where? When?

She didn't ask why.

Billy sat in his Escalade and told her everything he knew. He tried to be strong but was soon fighting back tears. The feeling had become all too familiar.

"I'll never forgive myself for getting Mark involved in this," he said.

There was a long silence. Anita was apparently searching for the right words. Oddly enough, she was trying to comfort *him*.

"Billy, he thought a lot of you and wanted to be involved," she said. "He was excited about the case, the most excited I've seen him in a long time."

"When was the last time you spoke with him?"

"Not since I talked to you last. I ended up taking care of that business myself. It was unusual not to hear from him, and that worried me. That's why I called you. But there were times like that through the years, where he was on a case and I didn't hear anything. It was usually a sign that Mark was getting close to wrapping things up. He'd just show up at the house and be done with it."

She began to cry softly.

Billy kept the phone to his ear and watched the coroner's men load Fletcher's body into the van across the way. Off to the side, the reporters were talking. They each nodded and Birchfield turned and walked toward the car.

The crying didn't last long. Anita Fletcher collected herself and her voice was strong again. Billy was amazed.

"There is one thing that may mean something to you," she said. "I noticed a strange text on my phone this morning, supposedly sent by Mark. It just looked like gibberish to me, like something that might have been sent by accident."

"What kind of gibberish?" Billy said.

"Some numbers and letters, all run together. I thought if it was important, he would have sent it to you."

"Can you forward that to me, Anita? I'm looking for anything to go on here. I promise you, I won't rest until I find out who did this."

"I know you won't, Billy, and I really appreciate you calling me. Hopefully we can talk again, after I've had some time. I don't know what I'll do without him ..."

Billy's eyes filled with tears again. This nightmare just didn't want to end.

"I'm so sorry," he said. "I'll be in touch soon. Goodbye, Anita."

Birchfield was waiting beside the car, and Billy motioned him in as he continued to stare at his phone.

"Hang on," he said. After a minute, it came up: 6000france04. Billy studied the line and shook his head.

"Help me here. This is a text Mark supposedly sent his wife sometime last night. Can you make any sense of it?"

Birchfield took a long look. "Well, you obviously have France. Maybe a street?" he said.

They each began to explore online.

"There is a France Road here," Birchfield said. "It runs along the Industrial Canal. Looks like a 6000 address, if that's what it is, would be pretty far down, way south of I-10."

"What about the last part? Oh-four."

"No idea, unless it's some sort of complex. Maybe a building number."

Billy plugged in the address on Google Maps. "Not much down there," he said. "Why don't we take a look after we finish here."

"You don't think this might be a setup? It just seems a little strange, a little too convenient."

"Could be, but everything about this seems like a setup. Let's find out. I owe it to Mark."

CHAPTER SIXTY-FOUR

Billy drove west in quiet reflection. He tried to recall Fletcher's last words to him, about the men the private investigator was supposed to meet that night.

Had he mentioned any names? Where was he meeting them? Had another meeting even been arranged?

"He was double-crossed, one way or another," Billy said, finally.

Birchfield looked over and nodded. He had also been mulling the possibilities.

"Showed up with a bunch of cash and ended up dead," he said. "Those guys could have done it on their own, or they could have told Romano about the earlier meeting, maybe to get back in his good graces."

"There's a strong possibility that somebody had been holding him for several days. They killed him last night and just dumped him in the park."

"So how would he have been able to text his wife? And why would he have texted her instead of you?"

"That's something else I can't explain. Maybe they were just messing with me, like putting my business cards in the pockets of dead people. We're not even sure if it means anything yet."

Billy took the exit and looped back toward the waterway. After a couple of miles, the state route dead-ended at France Road and he turned south. There had been a number of old businesses along the way, but they thinned out the farther he drove. By the time he was nearing the address he was looking for, it was mostly rundown buildings that were far removed from their productive years.

"Here it is," Birchfield said. "Six thousand."

Billy stopped the vehicle and they both stared across the large, desolate parking lot, which had a locked gate at the entrance to keep strangers out. Four metal buildings, in close proximity to each other and the canal behind. No vehicles that could be seen from their vantage point on the road. No signs of life.

Billy pulled onto the shoulder of the road and sat for a moment. Daylight was growing short, and in his current state of mind he wasn't sure what the smartest move would be. But he was in no mood to sit around thinking about it for long.

"Tell you what, Trey," he said. "I'm going back to that RV park that we passed just up the road. I'll park there and walk back to get a closer look at this place. There may not be anything to see, but I'll be thinking about it all night if I don't do it. It might be best if you just wait for me in the car. You can keep banging on that laptop."

Birchfield grinned. "And you're crazy, too. I didn't ride all the way down here to sit in the car. I'm with you."

Billy eased into a clearing in the overgrown RV park and turned off the engine. It was almost dark. For a moment, his mind drifted elsewhere. *Where had the good life gone? And why was he here, thinking about killing someone?*

"Ready?" Birchfield said.

"Almost."

Billy reached into the glove box and pulled out his Glock. "Now I am." Birchfield frowned but said nothing.

The land was flat and unobstructed back toward the industrial site. They could walk just off the road and not be seen. It would take ten to fifteen minutes to reach their destination.

For all practical purposes, the agent and reporter were still strangers trying to get to know each other. Some small talk helped ease the tension.

"You like working for a newspaper?" Billy said, just a minute into their walk.

"I do, but it's another one of those dying industries," Birchfield said. "Don't know how long I can keep doing it. It definitely won't be carrying me to retirement."

"That's a shame, too, because the stuff reporters dig up is more in demand than ever these days. It always seemed like a respectable business to me, when it's done right. But when the revenue streams dry up, I guess something has to give."

"Usually it's the people on the payroll. My father was a newspaperman, and he never would have imagined the business fading away like it has. It's old-school reporting, and nothing old school seems to work well anymore. What I like most about the job is the story always changes. Every day is different. Days like this are really different."

"I hope you have a prize-winning story to write when we're done here, Trey. With a happy ending, of course."

It was a clear night, and a full moon was already showing the way as they moved briskly along.

"So what about you?" Birchfield said. "You like being an agent?"

Billy chuckled. "I used to. I've loved sports my whole life, and the job suits my personality. It's fun and games, taken to a higher level. Things can get contentious, but I never dreamed I'd be dealing with the kind of problems I've had lately. Never dreamed I'd be walking through a field in New Orleans with a gun."

The old buildings were in sight. There was a tall chain-link fence surrounding the property, so they'd have to walk out to the road and slide through a narrow opening beside the guard shack. There didn't appear to be any security cameras at the entrance. A few lampposts illuminated the parking lot in front, but the buildings were dark.

"Let's go around back and see if anything is going on," Billy said.

They walked along the fence and turned the corner. Three vehicles suddenly came into view, parked under another lamppost beside the far building. Building number four, the large sign on the side said.

Billy dug the Glock out of his pocket and held up a hand. A lone figure was getting into one of the cars. The engine started and they had to duck behind a cluster of shrubs as the headlights swept across the lot.

"This could be the place," Birchfield said.

"I'm still afraid we might be walking into a trap. If we blow it now, everything goes up in smoke, including us."

"What should we do?"

"Well, we're seriously outgunned here," Billy said. "Maybe we should get the cops involved."

"It's definitely your call. I wouldn't mind having a bunch of armed professionals deal with this, but the cops down here are a different breed. A lot of them can't be trusted; that's what David Mettetal told me. He said there have been so many leaks when it comes to Romano, it's like everybody is on the take. They should have been able to throw him in prison a long time ago, but he's always one step ahead."

"Then let's learn what we can while we're here, hopefully without getting in too deep," Billy said. "We can move a little closer and see what we're up against."

The men crept along the edge of the building toward the parked vehicles. There wasn't much cover and they were exposed to anyone who might come along. Still, they pressed on.

The building had a metal entry door with a narrow window down the right side, and Billy approached the glass carefully with his gun drawn. Birchfield stood watch behind him.

Peering inside, Billy could see two men standing and talking in the distance. They were wearing dark windbreakers, and it was hard to tell if they were armed.

Were they Romano's men? Were they guarding something, or someone? Or were they just security guards keeping an eye on the place?

Billy walked back to Birchfield.

"I'd love to take a look around in there," he said. "But this probably isn't the time. Now that we've seen the layout, let's go back to the hotel and think about things. If we've found Jarvis, we'll know by this time tomorrow."

CHAPTER SIXTY-FIVE

illy was mulling over possible options when there came an excited knock at his hotel door. Birchfield entered with his Air Book in hand and a bemused look on his face.

"Let me show you something," he said, flipping open the laptop. "I was talking to David Mettetal again, and he was telling me he had done some more digging in their archives on Romano. Here."

The image on the screen showed a group of men in suits, standing, it appeared, on the steps of a courthouse. An attorney was addressing several media members who had gathered around.

"Any of this look familiar?" Birchfield asked.

Billy took a long look and shook his head. "Where is it?"

"Federal court, here. It was the end of the Allied Global Shipping trial back in 2012. I assume you remember that."

"Sure. I had already left the law firm in Atlanta by then, but I remember it well. Shipping fraud, organized crime. It had a lot of moving parts, and there was a lot of money involved. I know we got convictions."

"Well," Birchfield said, "the three guys behind the lawyer here were a big part of that operation. See the one on the right? He was the brains. Name was Anthony Matranga."

"I remember that now. Came from an old crime family in Sicily that had set up shop in New Orleans years ago. Why are you showing me this?"

"Because Matranga had a son who was already being schooled to take over the family business here. He ended up stepping right in when daddy went to jail. Has always used his mother's maiden name. Romano."

Billy's eyes grew wide. "So that's Frank Romano's father? Where is he now?"

"Died in the state pen about a year ago," Birchfield said. "Coincidentally, not long after that was when the stories about Junior started coming out. That's about the time Sonny Bradley's business really ramped up and he started chasing after players. And one in particular."

"How did you put all this together?" Billy said.

"It wasn't hard, just took a little digging online. Connecting the names was the toughest part. David Mettetal put me on the right path."

"So what should we make of it? I mean, how does it factor into Jarvis disappearing and everything that's been going on with me?"

"Seems pretty obvious now," Birchfield said. "This is all about revenge, Billy. Frank Romano is trying to ruin you, one blow at a time. Jarvis Thompson is the biggest blow, for sure, but only part of the plan. Romano corrupted your brother and your girlfriend. He's undermining your business and, really, your whole existence. I'm sure he won't be happy until you have nothing left."

Birchfield hesitated. "Then, who knows what he'll do. Of course, he could have already had you wiped out by now if he wanted. This is all just a twisted game to him."

Billy stood still for a moment and gave Birchfield a strange look, equal parts resolve and defiance.

"If that's true, he should have done it before I knew what was going on," he said. "I've never been a violent man, but I don't have a whole lot to lose at this point. I'll kill the son of a bitch if I get a chance. I owe it to John."

The sound of that made Birchfield visibly uncomfortable.

"I just want you to know, Trey, you don't have to be part of this," Billy said. "You're here to write a story, not chase criminals. This isn't your fight."

Suddenly that grin returned to the reporter's face.

"Maybe not," he said, "but I wouldn't miss it for the world. Let's go back out there tomorrow and see if we can't find what we're looking for."

CHAPTER SIXTY-SIX

A restless night had turned into a somber afternoon, and the men were unusually quiet as they climbed into the Escalade. Billy kept imagining the scene where this nightmare would end. He wasn't sure how, but Jarvis had waited long enough. All of them had.

They would make their move right after dusk.

Ever the enterprising reporter, Birchfield had been researching property records that morning and discovered that the warehouse buildings along the canal belonged to a company called Gulf Coast Cold Storage. The bulk of its business was blast freezing pork and poultry for export to Mexico. It once was the largest facility of its kind in the New Orleans area but hadn't been in operation for more than a decade.

That begged the question: What would be going on there now that required the constant attention of several men? The answer seemed obvious.

Next question: What if it was a setup? What if Romano's men had sent the text to Anita Fletcher, knowing she would pass it along to Billy? What if they were ready and waiting?

"We can still let the cops handle this," Birchfield said, breaking the silence as the men settled into their seats. Billy had never given up on the idea, but now he was almost amused at the thought of walking into the New Orleans Police Department and trying to explain this whole thing.

He decided it was time to press on with the mission at hand.

"It may be damn foolish," he said, "but I'm to the point where I'm ready to deal with Romano myself. He wanted to ruin me, to ruin Jarvis, and he's done a pretty good job up to now. Let's see how he handles the rest of it."

"These are people who are used to dealing with messy stuff like this," Birchfield said. "Are you afraid?"

"Not anymore."

Daylight was fading as Billy retraced his tracks of the prior night. Finally, he made the slow turn off the road and into the old campground.

The car had barely rolled to a stop by the time he opened the glove box and retrieved the gun. He pulled a loaded magazine from his pants pocket and popped it in place. Billy stared intently at Birchfield, as if giving him another chance to back out.

"Let's do it," Birchfield said, brandishing his own weapon from a backpack. Billy did a double take.

"You have a license for that?" he said.

"Sure do. I used to do a lot of shooting up in New York, just for fun. I don't think I've had this thing out more than twice since we moved to Tennessee, but I figured it might eventually come in handy on this trip. Two guns are better than one, right?"

"I know what your wife would say."

"Let's not tell her."

Within minutes they were back in position at the industrial complex. There were two vehicles parked there this time – both dark SUVs. For all they knew, the third could show up at any moment.

Billy had noticed the previous evening how the dimly lit building had large areas of shadows just inside the door. If they could slip in unnoticed, there were plenty of places to hide and prepare a surprise attack.

A day of thinking hadn't really yielded much of a plan. It had just given them time to muster all their nerve to take whatever action proved necessary. They knew things could get out of hand in a heartbeat. Birchfield just hoped he'd be the one to write the story.

The men were pondering the circumstances, crouched behind the same bushes and watching the entrance intently, when a rustling sound behind them broke their concentration. Before they had time to react, a dark figure appeared from nowhere, drawing a bead on them with an assault rifle.

"Drop the guns," came the voice. They did as they were told and put their hands in the air. For a moment, at least, they prepared to die.

The man looked like a ninja, dressed in black from head to toe, and walked up to them cautiously. He stopped a few feet away and ripped off the mask he was wearing.

"Hello, Billy," he said. "Long time no see."

Billy strained to recognize the face. Then it registered. "Dante?"

"You know this guy?" Birchfield said.

"It's Jarvis's brother … Jesus, man, you scared the hell out of us. How long have you been here?"

"I've been on the trail of these guys for almost a week now. If Jarvis is here, there's a whole lot of hell about to come down on their heads."

Dante surveyed the scene calmly.

"Let's hope we're at the right place at the right time," he said. "It doesn't look like anybody is expecting us. Go ahead and pick up your guns, and let's back away for a minute."

The men took cover and caught their collective breath. Billy hadn't seen Dante in years, since Jarvis left home for college. Mark Fletcher had tried to track him down in the days after Jarvis's disappearance but had no luck.

"What do you know about what's going on here?" Billy said.

"There are three guys inside, and two of them rotate in and out. One guy stands watch over in the far corner. I'm assuming Jarvis is being held in that storage area."

"So you haven't seen him?"

"No, but I was just getting ready to shoot my way in when you showed up. I believe I can kill all three before they know what hit them."

"It looks like you came prepared," Billy said.

"More prepared than you guys. You sure you're up for this?"

"We're sure. I'm pretty good with a gun."

"Do you know if Romano is here?" Birchfield said.

"These are just his thugs. He's probably in town having a nice meal somewhere. We're about to ruin his night."

Billy smiled. For the first time in weeks, he felt in control again.

"Let's see what the three of us might be able to do together," he said. "I like our chances."

CHAPTER SIXTY-SEVEN

The men crept to the entrance, and Billy slowly tested the knob. Unlocked. He opened the door just a crack and held his breath, waiting for any sort of alarm to sound. There was none.

The men slipped inside and toward the back wall of a huge freezer compartment. They had to make their way across an open area but were quickly enveloped by the shadows, perhaps thirty yards away.

The sound of voices could be heard over the constant whine of a couple of space heaters. They came from the far corner of the building, and Billy craned his neck to try to get a look. He could see the back of a man's head. Reddish, stringy hair. Tall.

The man turned and came into clear focus. Mean Gene, the sniper.

That likely meant Tommy was also on the scene, and it didn't take long to confirm. The hysterical laugh echoed from an office area out into the cavernous building. Only one man sounded like that. Tommy was going through his usual routine with another guard.

Billy sat still and considered this for a moment. It was three on three, and his team had the element of surprise. He knew all of Romano's men were surely well armed, but he hadn't seen any weapons out yet. If the intruders could catch them off guard, this might end without complete chaos.

On the other hand, things could go horribly wrong. But Billy was prepared to do whatever it took to free Jarvis. He thought of his father. If it was a question of kill or be killed, his mind was already made up.

Billy motioned Dante close and was reminded of what a big, muscular man Jarvis's brother was. He still looked like an athlete – one with a huge chip on his shoulder. Billy pointed to Gene and whispered, "Whatever happens, don't let him get off a shot." Then he went back to Birchfield. "We'll go around the corner and take care of the other two," he said. "Follow me, and stay down."

Just as they prepared to move, a cell phone rang and Tommy walked out of the office. He had his back to Billy and Birchfield, who had taken a position behind a rusted forklift that probably hadn't moved since the plant closed. The conversation lasted only a minute. It sounded like the boss was checking up on his henchmen and their prized prisoner.

"So Billy Beckett may pay us a visit?" Tommy said to no one in particular. "I don't think he's stupid enough to do that, especially after taking a ride with us, but we'll be looking for him."

Too late.

As Tommy stuck his phone back in his pocket, Billy took a deep breath and nodded to Birchfield. *Now!* Using the forklift as cover, they stood up and leveled their guns at Tommy.

"Police!" Billy yelled, without really thinking it through.

Tommy stood still, but Gene quickly reached for his gun and fire sprayed immediately from the barrel of Dante's AK-47. Gene fell hard against the wall, eyes wide, blood streaming across the floor in all directions. The insurgents had caught him by surprise.

The third man fired wildly from just inside the office door, and he, too, was cut down in a hail of bullets. He laid still in the doorway.

"Why don't I kill this one, too," Dante shouted, a crazed look on his face as he placed the rifle barrel against the back of Tommy's head. "Is this what you did to my father, little man?"

Tommy fell to his knees, seemingly resigned to his fate. "Please," he said.

"No, Dante," Billy said. "We need him. Trey, you keep him covered. If he moves, blow his head off."

Billy and Dante quickly stepped over Gene's lifeless body and tried to open the door he had been guarding. It was locked. They rolled the dead man over and dug the key out of his pocket. He held his breath as the knob turned and light streamed into the dark room.

There in the corner, dirty and exhausted, sat the football star everyone had been searching for. Jarvis looked up and just shook his head.

"It's over," Billy said as he knelt and wrapped his arms around his protégé in a long-awaited embrace. "It's finally over."

Dante kissed his brother's cheek and helped him to his feet, but Jarvis wasn't free just yet. He still had one ankle chained to the wall.

Billy walked back outside to where Tommy was face down on the floor.

"Tell you what, asshole," he said. "You're going to change places with our man here. Where's the key? And the phone, too, while you're at it."

Tommy tossed both out beside him and looked up at Billy. "You can't just leave me here," he said.

"Why not? We're leaving your best friends with you. And I'm sure somebody will be coming along for you soon."

Billy knelt down and released Jarvis, who leaned on his shoulder and limped unsteadily from the room. He glared at Tommy. The short man suddenly looked a whole lot smaller.

"Where's the appreciation?" Tommy said. "You know we could have taken any of you out anytime we wanted. But we didn't."

"You probably should have – and you would have if your boss had told you to. Now get up. Your room is ready."

"I've got a better idea," Dante said. "I'm going to put the cuffs on him and take him for a ride. He's going to show me where they buried my old man. Somebody has to pay for that, too."

"I don't know what you're talking about," Tommy said.

"You remember Charles, don't you? People in town said the last time anybody saw him, he was getting into a car with you and your friend over there. You're going to show me the grave, and hope I don't put you in a hole right beside him. I can't promise anything."

"Their boss said he was buried in a sugarcane field outside town," Jarvis said. "They killed him."

Billy nodded. "There's just one more little item of business here," he said, turning to Tommy. "Tell me where Romano is."

CHAPTER SIXTY-EIGHT

Before the answer could come, a man at the back door caught everyone by surprise. He was posing in the entranceway, a sawed-off shotgun braced against his shoulder. It was pointed at Billy.

"I guess this is the part where I say, freeze," the man said. "And, uh, drop those weapons."

Dante hesitated for a split second ... and then complied with the others. They all stood still, fixated on the tall stranger in the hooded sweatshirt. The tables had turned again, it seemed. *What now?*

The bearded man motioned them against the wall.

"Who are you?" Billy said.

"You asked for a Romano, and now you've got one. I was just stopping by to check on things, and glad I did. Looks like all hell has broken loose here. My father said you might come, but you were a little early. You obviously caught Gene over there by surprise, and that's not easy to do. Congratulations."

Paul looked down at the bodies on the floor and shook his head.

"A messy business, just like Dad said. Now kick those guns away, and don't do anything stupid. I don't want to have to kill anybody just yet."

"Paul Romano?" Billy said.

"That's right. We've never met, but I think we have a mutual friend. I know a lot about you, Billy Beckett."

"Wish I could say the same. Rachel never mentioned you."

"I'll bet not. She's a good girl, and there was never much to tell."

Paul eased out of the doorway with his eyes focused on the group. He reached out with his foot and slid the guns to the far wall.

"All right, gentlemen," he said, "toss your phones over there – I'm sure you've all got one – and let's walk into the football player's room. By the way, how were the accommodations, Jarvis?"

Jarvis kept his head down and hobbled toward the room, bracing himself against the wall. The others slowly began to follow.

"What are you planning to do here?" Billy said. "You don't want to make things worse than they already are."

"You're right. I want to make everything better for my father, and that means cleaning up this mess. There's a lot here that needs to disappear in a hurry."

Paul flashed that wicked Romano smile, causing Birchfield to look warily at Billy.

"Let me help," Tommy said, stepping away from the group. Paul quickly waved him back into line with the shotgun.

"Not this time, Tommy. You're going with the others. And that includes our dead friends here. Each of you, grab an arm."

The blood smeared across the floor as the bodies were dragged into the rear of the small room.

"Everybody back," Paul said. He reached up with the barrel of his gun, shattered the light bulb and closed the door. The men could hear the deadbolt engage. They were officially prisoners.

The windowless room was almost completely dark, except for small slivers of light that squeezed through cracks around the doorframe and illuminated their faces.

"Are you all right, Jarvis?" Dante said.

"No worse than I was. Been here, done that."

"Do you know of any way out of here?" Billy said.

"I was chained to the wall, so I didn't get to look around much."

"Good to hear you still have your sense of humor."

Billy turned toward Tommy in the darkness. "All right," he said, "let's hear it. How do we get out?"

"I'm not sure. I never spent much time in here."

"By the way, Romano's kid obviously thinks highly of you. He just threw you away like the piece of trash you are."

Tommy sighed.

"He's a lot like his father," he said, "but without the loyalty. He's crazier, more unpredictable. I've never trusted him, and I guess it works both ways."

Tommy paused. "He'll regret this."

Just outside the room, Paul had decided to take care of the situation himself. He walked back to one of the space heaters near the old loading dock and rolled it in front of the metal door where the men were trapped. He unscrewed the fuel cap and pushed the heater on its side. The kerosene spilled onto the floor and ignited immediately.

It wouldn't take long for the building – the whole complex – to be engulfed in flames. Investigators would need time to sort through the ashes, identify the remains and piece together the puzzle. By then, the Romanos would again be well out of reach.

Paul quickly made his way to the exit, stopping only briefly to glance back. He slipped out the door with an approving grin.

The smoke was beginning to thicken, and it was apparent to the men inside what was happening. They were going to be burned alive.

"It's now or never," Billy said. "Let's try to break the door, all at once."

"Wait," Tommy said. He walked over to the lock and pulled another key from his pocket. "Let's try this first."

After a few seconds, the door sprang open and the men spilled out of the room and into the growing inferno. Flames were already beginning to leap from the floor to the walls and furnishings nearby. The men covered their faces and ran toward the exit. Billy waved Jarvis and Dante to the side. He scooped up a couple of the guns on the way and yelled for Birchfield to get the phones.

In the mad dash outside, they saw the taillights of Paul's car in the distance, darting across the parking lot toward the entrance. He had waited just long enough to make sure the fire had spread. Now he was likely headed into town to tell his father of the heroic deed.

Tommy didn't hesitate in trying to make his own escape. He jumped into one of the SUVs, threw it into gear and sped straight toward the gate where Paul was standing, fumbling with his keys. For a brief moment, it looked like there were two figures in the shadows.

From behind, Dante opened fire as he ran across the parking lot. Tommy's vehicle swerved wildly at the entrance, the headlights offering one last glimpse of Paul, frozen with his arms outstretched. The SUV plowed over him before careening off the guard shack and rolling. The grinding sound of metal on pavement filled the night air.

Tommy had been ejected and was bleeding heavily when the men reached him.

"I told you he'd regret this," he said, cackling to himself.

Billy knelt down beside him as the orange glow in the distance grew brighter. "You have to tell us, Tommy. Where's Romano?"

CHAPTER SIXTY-NINE

The crime boss spent most of his time moving back and forth between the waterfront and several bars in the bowels of town that were under his control. He had learned the lifestyle from his father, how to lay low and still have a major presence on the streets.

The Polo Lounge was tucked away deep in the French Quarter, a dimly lit establishment at the far end of Perdido Street, and Billy could feel the foreboding the moment he walked in. He pulled his black jacket tight around his neck and approached the long bar, which was shrouded in cigarette smoke. A smattering of customers leaned over their drinks and stared into space, seemingly lost in thought. This wasn't a place for deep conversation.

The muscular bartender threw down a cocktail napkin in front of Billy, looked into his eyes and waited for a response.

"Jack Daniel's. Neat."

Billy stood at the bar and casually took inventory. He didn't immediately see anyone matching Frank Romano's description. Tommy had said that he was a large man with a goatee, the kind of man you wouldn't be inclined to just walk up to, and he'd have at least one of his guards close by.

The club was a two-story building that had the feel of a maze, with narrow hallways running off in all directions, so Romano could be anywhere. Billy figured he had a private space upstairs, and it seemed even more likely as he watched a server walk out of the small kitchen and head up with a tray of food.

The bartender set the glass of whiskey in front of Billy and began wiping his work area with a towel. His muscles bulged the way a bouncer's should.

"Hey man, I wonder if you might be able to help me," Billy said. The bartender kept wiping without as much as a glance. "I'm looking for someone who may be here. Frank Romano."

The man abruptly stopped what he was doing and glared at Billy with a healthy dose of suspicion, trying to judge exactly who he was dealing with.

"Never heard of him."

"Are you sure? I think he might want to talk to me."

"Who are you?"

"Billy Beckett. He'll know."

The bartender flipped the towel across his shoulder and walked down the corridor to where a man was standing at the bottom of a stairway. They whispered for a minute, and then he nodded to Billy to follow. Billy emptied his glass and slapped a ten on the bar.

"Save my change," he said. "I'll be back for more."

"I wouldn't count on it," the bartender said.

As he approached the guard, Billy was spun face-first to the wall and patted down with authority. "Easy now," he said. The guard showed no emotion and extended his arm toward the stairway.

"You first," he said.

They walked to the top of the steps, took a right turn and went down to a set of double doors. The man knocked, and there came a muffled response. He stuck his head in the room.

"Boss, there's a guy here asking about you. Says his name is Billy Beckett."

There was a pause and Billy was escorted in. Frank Romano was sitting in a large chair in the corner of the room, a tray of food in front of him. He looked at his visitor with a curious smile and lit a cigarette.

"Billy Beckett," he said. "Sit down. Please. It's okay, Mario, just wait outside."

Billy took a seat on the couch facing the crime boss.

"So we finally meet," Romano said. "I've heard a lot about you, and now here you are. I thought you might come to look for your friend, but not here. Do you know what you've gotten yourself into?"

"I think I do now," Billy said. "I must admit, Frank, it was a long time before I understood this game you've been playing with me."

"Game?"

"Jarvis Thompson. My brother. My girlfriend. I just couldn't figure why a big mafia boss like you, way down here in New Orleans, would be messing with a little sports agent from Tennessee."

The men studied each other carefully, and Romano took a long drag off his cigarette.

"You're not just a sports agent, though, are you?" he said. "You're an attorney."

"I used to be."

"That's right. And you were a good one, weren't you?"

"That's what they told me."

"Apparently you were smart enough to figure out a little scam that one of the shipping companies was running down here," Romano said. "You sent Anthony Matranga to prison. My father. Remember?"

"I remember," Billy said. "Two-bit crook that got in way over his head. I'll give him credit though; that scheme worked for a while. Made him lots of money."

"Two-bit crook?"

Romano's face hardened and his mood began to darken.

"My father ran the show in New Orleans," he said. "He was a great man, and you took away the last years of his life. There were others, of course. You probably heard about the prosecutor. He had a terrible accident not too long ago."

"I hadn't heard, actually."

"No matter. You're the one we're talking about here. There hasn't been a day go by since then that I haven't thought about you."

"So now you run the show in New Orleans? I have to tell you, Frank, I'm a little disappointed in the way you're conducting business. I shouldn't be standing here right now. Why am I not dead?"

"You're going to suffer until I decide it's time to put you out of your misery. You'll be begging me to kill you."

Billy smiled and shifted in his chair.

"Big man, that time is over," he said. "I just wanted to come here and tell you personally. You no longer control Jarvis Thompson, and you no longer control me. We went out to the warehouse tonight and freed him from your men. They didn't fare very well either."

"I don't believe you."

"Go ahead and call Tommy; that's his name, isn't it? Little guy with a funny laugh? See if he answers."

Romano picked up the phone on the table and fumbled to make the call. Suddenly a muffled ring came from Billy's waistband.

"Oh, this must be it," he said, pulling out Tommy's cell. "And by the way, I think Tommy ran over your son. Paul is dead. They all are."

Romano flew into a rage. He reached under the seat cushion and drew a pistol.

"Mario!" he yelled toward the door. There was no answer.

"Put that down, Frank," Billy said. "Mario isn't going to help you. The cops are probably here by now. Don't make things any worse for yourself."

Billy had become numb to fear, or maybe he was just out of his mind. But he stood slowly and faced Romano with an outstretched hand.

Suddenly the doors were kicked open.

"Police!"

Romano turned for an instant and Billy launched at him with everything he had, pinning the gun against Romano's chest. The men struggled, locked together, face to face. A shot rang out and they parted.

The cops who had flooded the room with their weapons drawn all froze. The crime boss fell limp to the floor, gasping for air. Blood gushed from a wound on the side of his neck.

"I should have killed you a long time ago," he said to Billy. His voice was fading, the breaths growing short. "I let you get too close."

"Yes, you did," Billy said.

Paramedics were on their way up, but an ambulance wouldn't be necessary. Frank Romano, the scourge of New Orleans, would be dead in a matter of minutes.

Billy rocked back onto the couch, rubbed his face and took a deep breath. He could feel the emotions of the last month all pouring out at once.

"Where are my friends?" he asked the officer in charge.

"They're both downstairs in a private dining area."

"Both?"

"Yeah, the football player seems to be okay, considering what he's been through. The reporter has just been sitting at a table with his laptop, typing away. We've all got a lot to talk about here."

Billy nodded solemnly. "Then it's time to go home."

CHAPTER SEVENTY

The digging was over. Police had found what they were looking for.

Detective Allary and several men in uniform were gathered around the site in the sugarcane field where Charles Ratliff had been buried, waiting for instructions from the forensic pathologist. The work lights cast an eerie glow on the scene at the crack of dawn.

The dead man's sons stood together silently in the distance, a few feet in front of Billy. Dante had an arm draped around Jarvis's shoulders. They had been interviewed by investigators and spent the last couple of hours at the hospital while doctors checked out Jarvis. His arm was in a cast, but he was cleared to go.

Neither had slept, and the strain of their ordeal was plainly evident on their faces.

"I'm sorry," Billy told the brothers.

Dante continued to stare at the gravesite. "He was a pitiful excuse for a father, but he didn't deserve to be executed like that."

"I'm sorry for John," Jarvis said. "Everything that happened … our father bears some responsibility. He helped bring those men into our lives."

The detective approached the group with a grim smile. He was pretty bleary-eyed himself.

"I hope there's a little closure for you here, gentlemen. There's a lot more to sort out at the warehouse site; our men are going to be there for quite a while. Is there anything more I can do here?"

"No, detective. Thank you," Billy said. "We're going to try to get a couple hours of sleep and head back to Tennessee. Three of us, anyway."

"Where's your reporter friend?"

"He stayed at the hotel to file his first story for his newspaper's website. That'll definitely have Knoxville buzzing this morning."

"It's going to be buzzing here, too," Allary said. "Frank Romano was a plague on this city for too long. I don't know how many times I thought we finally had him dead to rights. I wish you didn't have to be the one to deal with him at the end."

"Me too, detective."

Allary walked away and Billy turned to Dante.

"I didn't get a chance to ask earlier," he said, "but where were you when the police stormed the bar last night?"

"Outside, on the balcony."

"You mean, you saw everything that went on in that room? Why didn't you come in and help me?"

"I got there kind of late, and it looked like you had it covered. I didn't want to interrupt."

Dante smiled. "Jarvis, you've got a hell of an agent. I always said that."

CHAPTER SEVENTY-ONE

rey Birchfield's spread took up the whole front page of the *Knoxville Journal* and was packaged with a full-length picture of Billy and Jarvis walking arm in arm. Together again.

It was the lead story on the national news and would captivate the public for many days and weeks to come.

Billy sat on the veranda of his house and studied his image on the page. *Was that really me?*

"You said it'd be a hell of a story," said Birchfield, gazing down at the river from the veranda of Billy's house. "Some vacation, right?"

"It was a little more than we bargained for," Billy said. "I'm sure your bosses are jacked about the whole thing. They got the exclusive, and you're a media star."

"Yeah, but my wife is really pissed. You don't want to meet her right now."

They both chuckled.

"So what now for Jarvis?" Birchfield said.

"It'll be a little while before he heals, but he's young and strong. He'll stay with me here and we'll work to get him back in top shape for the combine. I don't know how all this will affect his draft position, but he's still a

great player, one of the best. Right now both of us just feel fortunate to have the opportunity."

"Hopefully he won't end up with the Saints, right?"

"Yeah, I think he's probably had enough of New Orleans to last him a while."

Birchfield smiled and stood. "What about his brother? Surely they'll be a little closer after what happened."

"We'll see," Billy said. "Dante may have a few legal problems to resolve before he's free and clear. And he said he wants to finish rehab, clean up his life. I'm going to do whatever I can to help him. Clarise is still in the picture, of course, which means all bets are off for the Thompson family."

"Good thing Jarvis has you looking out for him."

"Hey, what are agents for?"

Birchfield patted Billy on the shoulder and headed for the door.

"Call me again sometime," he said. "But no more road trips. Or shootouts."

Billy waved goodbye and turned instinctively toward the bar. The bottle of Jack Daniel's sitting on the counter was enticing. He studied it thoughtfully, and then placed it in the cabinet. Not today.

The news was spreading quickly, and reaction had been mostly encouraging. Most of the players, his guys, were still with him. That meant everything after so many personal losses.

Nothing else mattered at this moment.

Billy would try to immerse himself in the business again, refocus and take that next step. He knew they would all want to hear what he had to say.

EPILOGUE

Hope springs eternal on opening day, and nowhere was that more in evidence than Miami in early September.

The Dolphins were hosting the Carolina Panthers on a sun-drenched Sunday afternoon at Sun Life Stadium. An uncharacteristic buzz had been going through the famously distracted crowd since warm-ups, and it picked up as the teams took the field for the kickoff.

Wearing dark sunglasses and a solemn expression, Billy Beckett sat alone in a corner of owner Ernest Wolfe's luxury suite. He leaned close to the glass, his face resting in the palm of his right hand, and was deep in thought as he watched number eleven's every move.

The Dolphins had shocked many of the football experts three months earlier when they traded up – giving away a first-round pick, plus two later picks, to the Tennessee Titans – for the chance to take Jarvis Thompson second in the draft. They hadn't been scared away by all the negative publicity surrounding the wide receiver and made a bold move they hoped would reward the franchise and its fans for years to come.

It was time to see what they had bargained for.

The shocking end to Jarvis's college career had finally begun to fade. He had worked tirelessly all spring to get back in excellent shape, and there were no outward signs of his ordeal. Inside, no one could be sure.

All Billy knew was that a sense of renewal washed over them both. It was the first Sunday of the NFL season, and those big dreams were finally back on track. In Florida, no less.

The moment everyone was waiting for came early in the second quarter. Scoreless game. Dolphins with the ball at their own 37.

Quarterback Michael Brooks stood tall in the pocket and surveyed the field. Facing single coverage, his rookie receiver got half a step ahead on a post route, and Brooks lofted a perfect pass over the cornerback's left shoulder. Jarvis made a fingertip grab, shed the would-be tackler and never looked back. Seconds later he was standing in the end zone while the adoring Miami crowd saluted its newest hero.

Jarvis froze like a statue, his arms outstretched and his eyes turned toward the heavens as teammates mobbed him. High above, the ecstatic Dolphins owner went around slapping hands with everyone in sight.

As he jogged off the field with his first NFL trophy ball, the Autumn Blaze pointed to the luxury suite and flashed that confident smile.

Billy Beckett smiled right back.

###

Thank you for reading, and I sincerely hope you enjoyed *Deep Threat*. As an independently published author, I rely on you, the reader, to spread the word. So if you enjoyed the book, please tell your friends and family, and if it isn't too much trouble, I would appreciate a brief review on Amazon. Thanks again. My best to you and yours.

-Scott

ABOUT THE AUTHOR

Scott Pratt was born in South Haven, Michigan, and moved to Tennessee when he was thirteen years old. He was a veteran of the United States Air Force and held a Bachelor of Arts degree in English from East Tennessee State University and a Doctor of Jurisprudence from the University of Tennessee College of Law. He lived in Northeast Tennessee until his untimely death in November, 2018.

www.scottprattfiction.com

ALSO BY SCOTT PRATT

ABOUT THE AUTHOR

Kelly Hodge is a native of Johnson City, Tennessee. He graduated from East Tennessee State University with majors in communications and political science, and spent more than three decades in the newspaper industry as a writer and editor. He lives in the beautiful mountains of Northeast Tennessee

www.kellyhodge.squarespace.com

ALSO BY KELLY HODGE

Billy Beckett Book 2 (Fall 2019)

Made in the USA
Monee, IL
22 July 2021

74119883R10184